Never
too
Late

Laughing P

Book 3

Never too Late

Laughing P
Book 3
By Kari Holloway

This is a work of fiction. Any similarity between the characters and situations within its pages and places or persons, living or dead, is unintentional and coincidental

Paperback ISBN: 978-0-9993857-2-2

First edition 2017-edited by Beth Fred
Cover design 2017 by Steven Novak Illustrations

Current Edition: August 2017

Also by Kari Holloway

Laughing P Family
Cracked But Never Broken
Behind the Lens
Never too Late
Laughing P Collection Vol 1

Devil's Playground
Forgotten
Cry of Gold
Mark of Cain (Coming Soon)

For an updated list, visit
KariHolloway.com.

Dedication

To all the people who found me first and champion me on.

Chapter 1

"Payne! Get in here," Chief hollered from his office.

With a smile, I uncrossed my ankles, unfolded my arms, and pushed off from the concrete wall.

Jason exited the chief's office. He tossed a nod in my direction and disappeared into the kitchen at the opposite end of the hallway.

I rapped on the metal doorframe with my knuckles before entering the office.

Chief's office looked more like a kid's toy shop. Dogs pissing on fire hydrants and riding in fire trucks lined a shelf. Fire department patches from the different units he had served with laid upon fire department themed fabrics; each framed in their own plastic picture frame and hung on the wall.

"Chief." I nodded, as I sat in a chair.

"Payne. Your brother not budging?" His forearms rested against the calendar on his desk. Each day was marked in multicolored inks, every shift, secondary, and board meeting slanted sideways in his writing. He was the only other lefty I knew aside from Lexi.

"No, sir." I shook my head and sighed. I tucked a wayward strand of my brown hair behind my ear and reached for the hairband it escaped from, pulling it off and redoing my ponytail.

"I used to think you were the stubborn one. But the more you mellow, the more stubborn he becomes." He leaned against the back of his chair and laced his fingers across this stomach.

"Blame it on a woman," I muttered more to myself than the chief, thinking of Lexi.

"That's what a good woman does." He chuckled. His gaze went from me to his desk. He picked up the framed picture of his wife and him, running his thumb over the glass.

"Doesn't get easier does it, Chief?"

"Five years now. How's Maw-Payne doing?" He looked at me, as he set the frame back in its spot.

"About the same."

"Yep." He ran a hand through his short, grey hair. "It'll become normal in her own time. Not better or worse, just different." He took a sip of water and leveled his stare at me, switching to business. "Seeing how it's your brother's house, I shouldn't allow you to attend. But if I don't, you'll just show up anyway. Won't ya?"

"Yes, sir." I nodded with a tight-lipped smile.

Just because Damien was being an ass, it didn't mean I wanted him to be hurt … much.

"You can work first shift. Not the fire, but you can do the perimeter checks and keep him from walking into the house." He pointed a thick finger at me. "I mean it, Darien. I don't want to lose you over something like this."

"I understand, Chief." I held my hands up in surrender.

I'd spent the last few weeks caught between trying to talk Damien out of this and wanting to smash his face in with my fist. It was a fine line that blew with his attitude.

Chief motioned me out the door, and I wasted no time hightailing it to the kitchen.

The kitchen was just part of the great room. On the other end, a football game played on the big screen. Every volunteer firefighter, who didn't have a day job to attend, was here.

Lola smiled from the stove, hollering for us to fill up our plates and our tummies. The pan was a part of her as she flipped a pancake into the air, catching it in the skillet. She glided the other pan across the red-hot coil, rolling the sausages.

I joined the line of patrons circling the kitchen table. Piles of fluffy scrambled eggs and gravy filled my plate. I reached for a biscuit and lost the last golden one to a co-worker.

"Here you go, hun." Lola dropped a hot biscuit right on top of my plate, splattering gravy along my hand, before she refilled the basket on the table.

"Thanks, Lola." I smiled and nodded at her. I snatched a plastic fork from the red Solo cup and veered from the line of hungry people toward the television.

It was too early for a live game, but last night's Patriots' game played. Brady threw an interception, and those gathered around the flat screen erupted in a chorus of boos and cheers.

Chapter 2

The times of riding on the back end of fire trucks had passed, but on occasions like these, Chief still let us. All of first shift was dressed in turnout gear. Jason drove the big, red truck through the sleepy streets while Charles and I rode on the back. The cold morning air nipped at my cheeks, and despite the sense of foreboding that clung to my gut, I smiled.

The white brush truck, with its shiny new fire hose reels, followed behind us. Through the windshield I could make out Richard and Jeremy riding with their windows rolled down, and the reflective tape on their turnout gear broke up the dark Nomex fabric from the equally dark seats.

The wind blew through my hair, pulling the hairband loose. A piece of hair whipped back and smacked me in the eye. Reflexively I closed my stinging eye, and kept the other peeled for the familiar turn in the road.

The engine slowed and turned. Untouched frost acted like a blanket, tucking in the homes. Damien's house sat nestled in the middle of the block, framed by ice covered trees.

The truck rumbled to a stop near the red fire hydrant. Robotically, we set the chocks around the wheel, and I kicked them snugly against the rubber. One of the Hardys grabbed the coupling, an extra length of supply hose, and the hydrant bag before sprinting toward the iron hub.

I opened the back door and tossed my turnout jacket onto the seat. I grabbed my gloves from inside my helmet, shoving them in my pants pocket. The suspenders twisted, and I unkinked and adjusted the heavy straps, as I walked toward the ice-covered driveway.

It didn't surprise me to see Damien's dirty Chevy truck parked across the street from his home. He leaned against the dingy top coat, his arms crossed. Despite the cold weather, he was dressed in nothing more than a thin long-sleeve tee-shirt and a pair of jeans.

"Damien." I greeted him with a nod.

Nothing had been the same since that night in the Mistwood kitchen—hadn't been the same since he came home.

"Darien." He ran a hand through his hair, never taking his eyes from the beautiful two-story home.

Like a man trapped, he walked to the center of his yard, squaring off with the inanimate house.

I looked at him and the house. The blood-stained sheets and the dried rose petals were hard to erase from my mind, but I still didn't think burning the place down was the answer. I swallowed hard, as I remembered Lexi's screams on the surveillance system.

There were good memories here, just buried under a layer of fresh terror.

I cleared my throat and looked at the gathering crowd. Some peeked through curtains and others gawked from their front stoops. By the time the blaze was lit, they'd be pushing for a front row seat in the road.

He didn't blink.

"I'm making a pass." I left him staring at the house, unsure if anything I said made it through that thick skull of his.

Frost on the driveway crunched under my steps. I surveyed the area between the side of the house and the neighbor's yard. I trailed a hand alongside the plastic siding.

In the few years Damien had owned the house, the ranch hands and I had spent more time here than he had. Every ten days the front yard needed mowing, but underneath the spreading pecan and oak branches of the backyard, we could go a month or more before the grass reached above the top of my boots.

"You remember when we were playing football and couldn't figure out where Jackson threw that lateral?" Jason stood next to the air conditioning unit. "Found it." He pointed into the now bare spread of an oak branch that stretched toward the back room's window.

The football sat nestled in the net-like configuration of thin, crisscrossing twigs. Ice clung to the white laces.

"Damn." I reached for the tip of a branch and pulled it down. I wrapped my fingers around the ball, yanking it from its prison.

Once free, the branch bounced up and down before settling in with the breeze's movement.

I tossed the slightly deflated ball into the air and caught it single-handedly. The cold seeped into my fingers. On the next toss, I tossed the pigskin to Jason. "Your brother opening the windows?"

Before Jason could say something, the window in the master bedroom slammed open.

I gave a dismissive wave and rolled my eyes. With a nod, I continued the perimeter check, going over the area Jason had walked moments before.

Damien stood rooted in the spot where I had left him. His usually jolly expression was replaced with a constant look of stony acceptance.

I glanced between him and the house. Would resorting to this drastic act save him? Or was it a lie he was telling himself?

He didn't seem inclined to say anything, and I didn't know what to say to him. Some demons weren't ones we could share with others.

I squeezed his shoulder and checked in with Chief before making my rounds again.

Each time I made a pass, killing time before we reached that tipping point of no return, Damien crept closer to the porch. I shifted my weight and blew into my hands, breathing warmth to the tips. I should have grabbed the gloves Lexi had laid with my keys this morning.

The chilly morning refused to let go, as the sun rose, but once the blaze was set, no one would complain about Jack Frost.

Damien stood motionless. His jaw was clenched, and in his hand, he held a glass bottle with a white cloth shoved in the top.

"Damien, this is as asinine as ever. Let us do our job."

"I'm doing it my way. You just don't get it." Damien's green eyes glinted steel-like, and the anger housed within him was etched in the way he stood. He squared his shoulders, believing he was right in this insane plan of his.

I wasn't getting into this with him. It was his choice. He was as stubborn as a mule, and I'd learned in the years he had been gone not to argue so much with a brick wall—I wouldn't get anywhere.

He lit the cloth. The flame turned the white cloth black before the burnt threads drifted onto the crystal-covered grass at his feet. He pulled back his arm and tossed the bottle through the front window.

Time stopped. The rumble of the fire engine was mute. The wind didn't disturb a single leaf. Nothing dared to move.

I heard the crackle of the flame before the first signs of life wafted through the open windows. The smoke danced against the light-colored walls, rolled toward the ceiling, and caught in the cross-current of the open windows.

Damien didn't crack a smile. Instead he seemed lost in his own little world.

A few of my comrades circled the house, making sure the sparks didn't drift onto the fence and the neighboring buildings.

I twisted my gloves, the only thing keeping me from knocking sense into my brother.

"Go ahead, say it." Damien blinked before watching the fire climb higher.

"You didn't have to burn the house. You could have sold it." I unrolled my long shirt sleeves and rubbed my hands together to ease some the stiffness in my hands.

"You know how this town is. Even if some outsider bought it, it would always be remembered as the house where Ralph died. The house where Lexi was tortured." His voice trailed off.

Six months and he was still running. The house may not be here after today, but it would still stand tall in the town's memories.

I didn't need to be reminded what happened in this house. Not willing to fight with him, I walked toward the fire truck and my water bottle.

"Who gave him a Molotov?" I asked Chief.

"I did. And the Hardys." He leaned against the truck's pump panel.

I picked up my water bottle and turned around to watch the fire. I drank half the bottle.

Watching the fire move through the house, it made sense that Chief had given the fire a little more help than Damien's initial bottle. "What's the real reason you let him do this?"

"He was going to do it anyway. I'd rather have us on scene than him do it while drunk." Chief checked the gauges.

I didn't have anything to say.

I set the plastic bottle in my hat and trudged back toward Damien.

He studied me, and my stomach knotted. He sucked on the inside of his gaunt cheek.

"Can I ask you a question?" His gaze bore into me. "Do you love Lexi?"

My brow wrinkled, as I tried to figure out where this was coming from. The answer was easy.

A large beam fell inside the house and the sky wore a short eruption of embers.

"It's not that complicated of a question. Yes or no?" He exhaled sharply.

He wasn't going to like this. There wasn't a doubt in my mind.

"It's more complicated than just a yes or no. You don't mean do I love Lexi. You want to know if I love her, like a man should love a woman." I ran my hand through my hair and tried to put into words what I meant. "But yes, I love her."

I tensed waiting for the proverbial other shoe to drop.

He nodded and faced the house once more. His skin flushed from the heat. His hair was stringy and clumped with sweat.

The adrenaline began to wear off and the slam of a tailgate drew me from Damien's toxic bubble.

Red stood at the back of his truck, moving and arranging Maw-Payne's signature potluck dishes.

Preferring the company of less depressing people, I walked toward Red and greeted the old man.

"He ain't walked in there yet?" Red searched his coat pockets for his pack of cigarettes. He tapped one out and put it to his lips.

"Not yet." I glanced over my shoulder to make sure Damien was still affixed to the spot.

Turning to face Red again, the most stunning woman I'd ever seen, with long brunette hair, caught my attention. I smiled, as she was lost behind the viewfinder of her camera.

"Here. I'm sure she could use some hot chocolate." Red reached for a thermos.

"Only if it has marshmallows."

Red looked at me funny, like he knew a secret, but dug in the bag of extras Maw-Payne had packed. He tossed me the clear bag of mini marshmallows before pouring coffee for one of the firefighters.

I balanced two cups on the truck bed's side rail and poured the steaming hot chocolate into the tiny cups. I tore a hole in the plastic bag and dropped a few puffy blobs on top of Lexi's second favorite drink—the first being sweet tea.

Lexi's gaze was locked to the branches above her head. The lens in her hand extended, and she carefully focused before pressing the shutter.

A smile blossomed on her face as she pivoted toward me.

"Lex. Red told me you were here. I …" Some days I couldn't put two thoughts together around her.

"I didn't want to intrude on your job. I was just getting some shots and stuff." She waved the camera around in her hand, and the strap yanked on her neck, jarring her forward.

"You okay?" I chuckled and leaned down to gaze into her sea-green eyes, but she desperately tried to hide her embarrassment.

"I'm fine." She nibbled on her bottom lip and tried to suppress the chuckle that escaped. "It was a little funny, wasn't it?" She broke into a full laugh that came from her soul.

It was hard to not join in with the laughter. I offered her a cup of hot chocolate and a smile.

She peered into her cup and swished the contents around before taking a sip.

"The next crew should be coming on soon. Why don't you hang out and give me a ride home?" I dragged my fingers through my hair and scrunched it into a ponytail. "You wouldn't happen to have another band on you, would you? Mine broke." I held up the poor excuse of a hairband.

She dug into her front pocket and produced a handful of the elastic circles.

I picked one up, shaking the extras back into her hand. I swept my shoulder length hair into a sloppy ponytail and wrapped the hairband around the handful.

We turned to watch the house become nothing more than a burned-out husk of its self.

Chapter 3

Shadow, Lexi's newest German shepherd puppy, kept his nose glued to the rim of the picnic basket we'd gotten from Maw-Payne.

Unlike the Laughing P's long driveway flanked with fields of wheat and rye, Mistwood's driveway curved beneath the widespread oak trees, and the sun left dappled pools of light where it could. The homestead was just as different as the driveway itself. The Mistwood was a simple three-bedroom, two-bath stone house nestled in the woods, like Little Red Riding Hood's grandmother's home.

Shadow barreled over Lexi and out the passenger door. Like clockwork, he went to the barn, sniffing along the door base and following along the concrete showers toward the high-tensile fence line.

Lexi followed me along the paver path to the front door, and with a smooth turn of the knob, the never-locked door swung open. She squeezed by with the wicker basket.

I dropped my truck keys on the side table and turned on the floor lamp. "I'll bring in some wood." I grabbed the canvas tote beside the fireplace and headed for the side of the house.

The firewood rack was brimming with wood. My fingers scraped against the bark of a scrawny log. Bouncing the end up and down as I thought, I tried to remember if we were due snow or not. I tossed the log onto the growing pile, and pulled the blue tarp down over the stacked logs. I didn't relish the thought of prying frozen logs apart.

The screen door slammed shut behind me, as I bounced the load against my leg and maneuvered in the narrow space of the living room. I dropped the bag next to the fireplace and reached for the long matches on the narrow mantel. Kneeling, I struck the match against the striker plate and set the flame to the kindling I had set in the fireplace the last time we had thought about having a fire.

Shadow barked from the hallway for his nightly reward.

"How'd he do, this time?" I picked up a thin piece of wood from the floor and fed it to the flame.

Lexi was training Shadow to search each room when we got home. I had never thought about the amount of work that went into training a dog but she made it look easy.

"He did well." Her boots scraped against the uneven floor, as she moved into the kitchen.

I stood and stretched. "I've got to get my gear. Do you need anything out of the truck?" I checked my pockets for my keys before picking them from the side table.

"My camera's on the floorboard. If you're hungry, I'll see what Maw-Payne packed." She leaned over the back of the couch, hunting for the remote sitting on top of the television.

"Nah, I want to shower first." I was still full of Maw-Payne's delicious cookies.

Shadow beat his tail against the ground. His tongue hung from the side of his mouth.

"Well, go on, dog." Lexi smiled and gave a nod toward the door.

I held open the screen door and let the dog go ahead of me.

Shadow darted in the direction of the holiday tree—Lexi's version of a Christmas tree laden with food for the critters around the house. He sniffed around the base, blending in with the shadows. He popped up with a yellow tennis ball in his black muzzle and padded over to me.

"Tennis? Didn't you get enough exercise today?" I chuckled, as I pulled the ball from his jaws.

He balanced on his hind legs. His tongue dangled from the side of his mouth.

I tossed the ball, and he eagerly chased it. After a few throws, I grabbed the tennis racket off the back deck and whacked the ball further across the yard.

Not slowing down, Shadow sprinted after the ball, catching most of the long hits before the ball even had a chance to bounce. He trotted back and sat.

I rolled my shoulder, easing the burn that came from this exaggerated game of catch. "A few more, Shadow."

Shadow dropped the ball and bounded toward the front door. The urgency of his stride sent me on his heels.

Lexi was frozen at the kitchen sink. Her fingers tightened against the glass in her hand, turning her knuckles white. Her shoulders rocked as she timed her breaths. Yet a hint of panic clung to her as she shivered.

I wrapped my arms around her, pulling her back against me. She jerked for a second before settling against me with a sigh. A tear rolled down her sun-kissed cheek and dropped on my sleeve, creating a perfect dark circle against the dirty and dingy fabric.

"Lex, how about you take a shower while I get dinner plated?" I stared at the pictures on her walls. Joyful times stared back at me.

I hated seeing her battling the demons she carried around. She fought hard and faced everything thrown at her with a passion that she would overcome it. But even that approach left scars.

"You called dibs first. Besides, I got to check on the chickens and get the laundry together."

I could have called bullshit. Laundry was an excuse.

"I'll check the chickens. I got to fill the bird feeders, anyhow." I playfully swatted her butt, sending her down the hallway toward the master bathroom.

"Fine. I know when I'm outclassed. I think you just like smelling like smoke." She chuckled before disappearing into her room for pajamas.

Satisfied she wasn't going to double back, I slid the picnic basket across the plywood bar top and turned around to start the coffee pot.

Rushing into the laundry room, I snatched the bag of bird feed from behind the door and hastily filled the feeders before returning to the kitchen.

I opened the fridge, reached behind the bagged salad mixes, and removed the bowl of dough I had set to rise this morning. A few spices removed from the spice cabinet and the mix of brown sugar and sugar left in a covered bowl, and I was ready to make Lexi's favorite food, cinnamon rolls. Lexi couldn't resist fluffy rolls drizzled with cream cheese frosting.

The pipes in the wall vibrated and hummed, as the shower ran. This house had more noises than Maw-Payne's cracking joints made in a day.

I turned the ladybug timer on and set the pan of rolls into the oven. Glancing down at my shirt, flour and sugar clung to the textured fabrics. I pulled the dirty shirt over my head, and tossed it into the dirty clothes basket under the makeshift bar.

I dropped a couple of ounces of cream cheese in the mixing bowl. While waiting for it to soften a little, I leaned against the counter.

Shadow lay on the knotted floor mat in front of the kitchen sink.

I walked down the hallway and into the master bedroom. I'd lived in this room for four years, but the room seemed caught between Lexi's grandparents' designs and my unwillingness to claim it.

I pulled my boots off and dropped them by the door. My socks lay discarded on the worn, brown carpet.

The *thud* of a dropped shampoo bottle drew my attention to the closed bathroom door. As the only functioning bathroom since a tree crashed through the roof in the last storm, it was a tantalizing endeavor to keep on the right side of that door when she was in there.

Shadow scratched at the door. He pawed at the door handle and pleaded with his large black eyes to let him in.

I shrugged. *Why not?*

The latch clicked, as I turned the doorknob. Steam engulfed the room, and I had no doubt she had the shower as hot as the tankless water heater would allow.

Shadow padded along the black slate, his nails *clacking* with each step. He lay upon the bath mat, tucking his nose beneath this tail. His black fur stood out against the cream rectangle and disappeared against the slate.

Through the glass shower doors, Lexi ran her hands through her hair. The water pelted her breasts. Even though the glass was fogged, it didn't detract from the beauty of her curves, or the uncomfortableness growing in my jeans.

She dragged her hand across her face, clearing the water clinging to her long lashes. The only hint, besides the décor, that a woman lived in here was the bubblegum-pink poof. She rubbed the blue bar of Zest across the netting and began to coat her tan skin in cleansing soap bubbles.

I couldn't stand here, gawking at her. I pulled the door to, and staunched a cuss word that tried to pass my lips, as the rug in front of the vanity caught in the underside of the door. Wary of her catching me in a room I shouldn't be in, I left the door alone and padded back to the kitchen to finish the cream cheese frosting.

The spoon smashed the frosting against the side of the bowl, blending the ingredients smooth. I picked up the spoon and watched as the icing coiled and merged with what was left in the bowl.

Lexi's footsteps sounded against the floor.

"Feel better?" I could feel her eyes tracing the lines of my back.

"Yes. I didn't know Maw-Payne had packed cinnamon rolls."

"She didn't." I turned toward her and smiled in appreciation at how well my Bronco's tee-shirt clung to her frame. "I figured we might like dessert first."

Chapter 4

I set the last box of Christmas decorations in the living room, between the shopping bags full of new decorations and ribbon reels.

Monica, my charming and bossy sister, had lids off a half-a-dozen red totes and wouldn't let anyone touch anything until she compared thingamabobs and doodads to the idea bobbing around in her head. We'd be lucky to even get lights on the tree today.

Maw-Payne sat in her rocker. Monica's twins, Ethan and Julie, sat in her lap. The duo giggled and reached at the toy Maw-Payne twirled between her fingers.

I settled my Stetson on my head. Leaning over, I kissed Maw-Payne on the cheek and headed for the barn.

"Darien. Where are you going?" Monica leaned over a tote, red and gold tinsel dangled from her grasp.

"I've got something else to do." I grinned and winked.

Maw-Payne chuckled behind her wrinkled hand and swatted me on my way.

Lexi and Red were gearing up for horse retrieval for the guests Monica had coming for the holiday season. I chuckled at the little white lie we had perpetrated. If only everything else went as planned.

Lexi dragged the red handled curry brush along Regan's back. My horse turned her head, and Lexi leaned toward her muzzle, talking in low tones and smiling.

I was glad she didn't get teary eyed when she saddled to ride anymore. Losing Trigger this summer had been hard, made even more difficult by the circumstances.

Lexi set the saddle along Regan's back and waited for the horse to exhale before she yanked the straps tighter.

I tugged on her shirt sleeve and ducked to the other side.

Her braid whipped around, as she automatically looked at where I should have been. She laughed. "Ren, what are you doing here?" Her eyebrow rose in familiar suspicion.

"Getting you to laugh." I smiled and cocked my head.

She had a piece of straw clinging to her dark hair.

I reached up, pulled it free, and watched it spiral down to the ground.

"Come on." I wrapped my hand around hers and relaxed at the instant comfort that stemmed from our connection.

I led her past the barn to the small quarantine building. We didn't keep much in here: spare grains, saddles, broken tools we always claimed we'd fix but never did.

I settled my hands on her shoulders and maneuvered her for a perfect view of the large door.

"Close your eyes." I grinned, as anticipation built in me.

Without a protest, she closed those beautiful eyes of hers.

I glanced behind to see her turning her head to follow every bit of noise. The barn door caught against the ground, and I had to pick up the end to finish swinging it open.

The light inside was partial at best. Following the sounds, I walked down the wood-chip lined corridor to the last stall.

The filly reached her head over the half door, obscuring the sunlight that came from the open split door on the other side of her stall.

"Hey there, pretty girl." I rubbed her forehead and up behind her ears. "You ready to go meet Lex? She's going to fall in love with you."

I grasped the nylon lead and clasped it to her halter before I opened the door.

Lexi stood where I left her. Her eyes were closed, and she shivered as the wind danced around her, whipping the short, broken strands of hair along her neck. She pulled a string of hair out of her mouth and licked her lips.

"If you shiver anymore, I'm going to be cold." I laughed.

The filly nudged my shoulder.

"Okay, you can open them."

She gravitated toward the horse. Pure joy filled her gaze, and happiness radiated from her.

"She's beautiful!" She gasped.

"I was gonna surprise you on the solstice, but she hates being alone." I adjusted the brim of my hat, and my ears burned in pride.

"What's her name?" Lexi scratched the horse's ear.

"She doesn't have one. The Wundts hadn't properly named her yet." I held out my hand, offering Lexi a sugar cube.

The Wundts were the only ranch in a two-hundred-mile radius that raised Missouri Trotters. Even the Laughing P preferred Paints and Quarter horses. And every horse they raised had a five-word German origin pedigreed name that only they could pronounce correctly.

Lexi clicked her tongue and led the horse into the small corral.

I watched the three-year-old filly prance and turn, willingly trotting around the enclosure at Lexi's encouragement. Her chocolate coat glistened, and I thought all the hard work I'd put into sneaking off the last few days to groom the horse had been worth every crappy excuse I'd had to come up with.

"Thank you, Ren. She's beautiful." Lexi's voice cracked, as her throat tightened. "She reminds me of Trigger, but in a good way."

"She should, Lex. She's Trigger's great-great-granddaughter." I counted on fingers, making sure I counted the right number of greats.

With a shrug, I sat my hat on a corral post, pulled the sliding hairband out of my hair, and finger combed my unruly hair into a messy bun. I resettled my Stetson, and the horse tried stealing it off my head.

"Give me that." I chuckled at the playful horse.

Lexi threw her arms around me.

I wrapped my arms around her, anchoring her close. My voice caught in my throat as I felt every soft curve, I so badly wanted to run my fingers over, slide down my body.

Her eyes were the prettiest green. She blinked, and I followed the line of her long lashes above her rosy cheeks and to her unpainted lips.

I stared into her sea-green eyes and became lost in her happiness. I was finally going to kiss her; something I had wanted to do for longer than I could remember.

I leaned down, and the filly shoved us with her shoulder, sending both of us to the ground in a tangled mess of limbs.

With the moment lost, I stood and retrieved my hat. "Now we've got two strong-willed critters." I knocked my hat against my knee and looked at Lexi.

Lexi seemed unaware of the need coursing through me, and she talked to the filly. She flipped her braid over her shoulder, grasped the horse's halter, and led her to the main barn.

She was happy and that was enough for me.

Chapter 5

With Lexi off with Red, gathering the horses, I sat in the Laughing P living room, pulling on another strand of tangled lights from the tote. Why didn't we use the plastic holders Mira bought for the bulbs last year?

I plugged in the string of lights and hung my head. How could bulbs burn out when they weren't used that often? I straddled the rocking ottoman and began the tedious task of untangling the cords and replacing every burnt bulb.

Julie held onto the side of a tote, peering inside at the wooden train set all the Payne children had played with under the Christmas tree. She pointed inside and babbled at Ethan.

Ethan refused to move from his spot on the rug, playing with his toy truck.

Julie looked at the train and back at Ethan. She took a sideways step and then another. She let go of the tote and grinned. She gazed around the room and tried another step. She teetered for a second before she tried another. She fell back on her bottom. Musical laughter escaped through her rosy cheeks as she found the entire situation funny.

The front door opened. Jeremy walked in, looked at the pile of lights around my feet, and smirked. "Tree's ready," he told Monica.

"Thanks. Can you move those boxes over there, and how about that chair? Do you think it could go there?" Monica pointed around the room, as she spoke.

"I think the tree will be fine in the corner like it has been every year, child." Maw-Payne walked slowly to her chair. She squeezed her eyes shut as she sat.

"I'll get some more firewood. And then we'll move the boxes after the lights are on the tree." Jeremy nodded and headed out the front door and around the house to the firewood racks, unwilling to cross the minefield of a living room and the haphazard decorations again.

I scratched my beard and leaned over for my coffee cup. I swirled the last of the beverage around the cup before finishing it in a single gulp. I dropped the finished strand of lights to the side and headed toward the kitchen.

"Darien," Maw-Payne said.

I paused.

"Where's your brother at?" She whispered, as she laid her hand on my arm.

"I'm not sure. He was in here when I started on the lights." I glanced at the mantel clock. "That was an hour ago. I'll go find him." I patted her hand and smiled.

She slowly nodded and seemed to turn more toward her thoughts than the happenings in the room.

I set my coffee cup on the kitchen table and headed toward the office. The holiday music flooded the first floor, and I chuckled, as Monica voiced her opinion about the Hardys' selection. The brothers had played that CD on repeat to the point I refused to ride with either of them.

Out of habit, I peered into Maw-Payne's room. Granddaddy's pipes still lined the dresser. The last pack of flavored tobacco leaned against the wooden bowl I had made him when I got sober.

I scrunched my nose, chasing the memory and the loss from my thoughts. I rapped my knuckles on the office door. Not waiting for a reply, I opened it and went inside.

Damien reclined in the office chair with his boots crossed on top of the desk. His hair was longer than it had been in years, but still rather short compared to my own. I had thought him thin at the fire, but sitting in the chair dad had occupied so many days, he looked plain frail.

"Really, Damien?" I ran a hand through my hair, aggravated with my brother's continual disregard of everything. "Maw-Payne is asking about you. Can't you spend one day doing something useful?"

"There's bills that need paid." He reached for his Coke and took a swig.

The dark liquid sloshed around the clear bottle before settling.

"Monica took care of the bills at the first of the month. The same thing she's done since this summer, and the same way dad and Granddaddy did things." I intentionally left Lexi from the list.

"Contracts then." He waved me off, like a fly buzzing around his head.

"Ronald has all the contracts. Maw-Payne already took care of them. You can keep finding excuses until you're dead. Now all Maw-Payne wants is for you to join us decorating the tree, and this time, try to actually participate." I walked to the living room, forgetting my cup of coffee in the kitchen.

Jason settled the massive tree in the corner of the room. He glanced at Monica and Maw-Payne, and at their nod, he left the tree where it was.

Jeremy stood behind the women and stuck bunny finger ears behind my sister.

I took a step and snickered, as I popped Jeremy in the back of the head. "You do it like this." I raised my hands to resemble a moose rack and laughter filled the room.

Monica turned toward me and narrowed her eyes at me. But Maw-Payne's soft chuckle broke Monica's stern gaze into a warm smile.

Monica waved me off with a dusting rag in hand and turned to arranging a garland strand upon the mantel. Red and gold decorations and bows stood out against the green pine needles.

I settled in on the ottoman and watched, as Monica crowded the branches with little colored ornaments. By the time she was done, there would not be a shelf or doorframe left unadorned.

She paused at a shoe box she opened. She carefully removed the crinkled newspaper and held up the tiny penguin ornaments Granddaddy had gotten Maw-Payne every solstice.

Maw-Payne smiled, and her face looked younger. She delicately fingered the ornaments Monica held toward her. With a nod of approval, Monica hung the ornaments among the slightly bowing branches.

A weight against my leg made me glance down into Julie's brown eyes. She yawned, as I picked her up and held her. She nuzzled against my jaw and stroked my beard. Her free hand gripped my shirt. I patted her bottom and stepped around the scattered decorations.

During the day, the twins took naps in Maw-Payne's room, and that's where I headed now. I laid Julie down on Maw-Payne's quilt.

She moved her head. Her little hand reached out for her bunny and pulled it close. Unlike Ethan, she didn't care if she was alone or not.

I eased out of the room as Monica brought in Ethan who hollered and cried until he saw his sister already sound asleep in the big bed.

Something made me pause for a second and peer at the tiny duo.

"I know that look Darien. You'll get your happily-ever-after, and enjoy it while you can. Those two look innocent, but they ain't." She gave me a sideways hug and leaned her head against my shoulder.

I smiled softly at the thought of my kids having their mother's soft smile, straight dark brown hair, and the sea-green eyes that radiated kindness.

"Come on, sis." I led her back down the hallway and stepped into the living room.

The Christmas tree filled the corner of the room. The evergreen branches obscured part of the window. The fire light glinted on the ornaments and strings of white lights glowed.

Last year's solstice photograph sat on the mantel flanked by a tapered candle that flickered.

I moved around the cluttered room and touched the glass with my fingers. This would be the first Christmas without Granddaddy.

I miss you.

The back door slammed, and the ancient CD player skipped.

I turned and surveyed the room.

Jeremy mouthed, "Damien," nodding toward the back door before shoving the lid on another tote.

I followed him, grabbing my hat from the coat rack near the back door. Settling my hat on my head, I looked across the yard and noticed a trail of dust rolling along the field.

"Red and Lexi are back," I hollered as I opened the back door.

Chapter 6

Red and Lexi moved the herd of horses, cresting the rise and funneling them through the gate, into the fenced-in garden. The dapple and solid-colored horses spread out among the leftover vegetables. Some trotted a few paces with their tails raised, nickering to their comrades.

Lexi, aboard Regan, adjusted her hat and put heels to my Quarter horse's sides. With just a little nudge, Regan bounded across the field. She was a natural in the saddle, and Regan loved her as much as I did.

A few of the horses joined in with the spur of the moment gallop. Down the fence line the procession went followed by a thundering of hooves that the sky above never could compete with.

I reached down and scratched Shadow's ear, curious as to where the furball had been hiding.

The familiar *flop* of Buddy's long ears accompanied the ancient hound plodding from the open barn door.

I scratched Buddy's ear, flopping it over his head and down again. "Hey there. Were you lying in the barn office again?"

Buddy shook his head. His brown ears smacking the top and bottom of his head. Drool accompanied his shake, leaving a slimy substance caking my jeans and a wet trail across Shadow's face.

The heavy, quick clop of hooves ceased.

I looked up from the dogs to see Lexi's carefree smile fall to a tight-lipped line. Her fingers tightened on the reins, and she turned Regan from the gate.

Damien leaned on the pole gate with a smug look on his face.

I eased around Red and his stubborn horse, Edgar, coming through the gate. A lassoed solid-colored mare followed behind.

"Stay away from her." I shoved Damien.

He took a step back from the gate. "What you going to do about it? Same thing you did last time?" He taunted.

My hand tightened into a fist. I counted slowly to ten.

The last time I squared off against him had been that night on the Mistwood when Lexi rejected his proposal and ultimately their disproportionate relationship.

I shouldn't have left the room that night. The crashing of knickknacks that night had drawn me back inside the house to witness Damien's hands gripping Lexi's arms hard enough to draw blood. The look in her eyes and the soft pleading not to hurt him had been his only saving grace that night, and I wasn't sure how much further that grace would stretch.

I tightened my fingers in the front of his jacket. "Lexi doesn't need saving. She just doesn't need to get her hands dirty with the trash. Stay away from her."

I shoved him back against the fence post and headed toward the barn.

Over and over, I reminded myself that punching his lights out wouldn't solve anything.

Lexi grunted, settling on a hay bale. The liniment ointment bottle sat between her knees.

And thoughts of Damien got pushed to the back burner.

"What's going on?" I leaned against the doorjamb, trying to avoid blocking the sunlight that stretched into the saddling area.

"That damn mare thought Regan would roll over—while I was in the saddle." She winced as her fingers dug too hard along her wrist.

The heavy stench of the ointment overwhelmed the usually sweet scent of hay and the musky smell of horse and leathers.

"I'm fine, before you ask. Got a question. Who pulled the horses for the guests?" She glanced between Red and me.

"I'm not sure. It wasn't me." I came closer and held my hand out for the bottle.

She pretended not to notice.

I wiggled my fingers until she huffed and handed me the bottle.

I hated this stuff. The white liquid coated the sides of the glass as I rotated it. "Why don't you take the evening off? And I'll rub you down wherever you need?" I knew she wouldn't take me up on the offer, but I couldn't stop making her blush.

Chapter 7

I dragged the hand planer against the board. The repetition usually calmed my mind, but the longer Lexi and I cohabitated, spending more nights platonically in bed than not, the less soothing working in Sawyer's woodshop became.

"So, let me get this straight. You've told your brother that you're in love with Lexi and have been for over a decade. But you have no idea how she feels about you. Boy, do you have blinders on?" Sawyer looked among the sanding blocks and strips of sandpaper for his safety glasses that were on top of his head.

"It's more complicated than that." I didn't have any doubt she was attracted to me, but with our past, was I just a rebound? I shook my head, chasing that depressing thought away. If I believed that, I wouldn't be in Sawyer's shop at all hours of the night.

"Oh! Is that what kept you from beating Damien to a pulp after he trashed the kitchen?"

"How did you hear that?"

"He was at the bar, drowning his sorrows."

"Yeah, complicated." I didn't lay Damien out for the simple fact Lexi didn't want to be rescued and Maw-Payne wanted her grandkids around. If I did more than scuffle with him, I'd be disappointing the two most important people in my life.

"Did Dominick ever tell you how he convinced Mawve to marry him?" Sawyer reached on top of his head and smirked at finding his glasses.

I shook my head and set the planer down.

Sawyer tapped a pencil against the board before drawing a line. The tape measure chased the yellow tape and flipped off the end of the board. He moved the board through the table saw and picked up the two pieces, surveying their edges.

I waited for Sawyer to continue.

He was in his early eighties, up there with Pritchard and Granddaddy. Age had been kind to him. He still had a head full of hair, crows' feet gathered at the corner of his sharp eyes when he laughed, and he could move better than some people in their forties with both their legs.

"Dominick showed her the house—the one y'all live in. He told her, he'd add as many rooms as she wanted, if she would marry him. She told him to do it first, and that she wanted window boxes on every window too." Sawyer picked up the glue and ran a line along the joints.

I passed him a long clamp.

He set the level on the four sides, hammered the joints together, and began sliding the clamp tight. "Well, Dominick didn't know much about building a house, so he gathered all his friends together. All winter long, from snow and ice to the pretty blue skies, we added a second floor." He smirked, as he reminisced. "I had never seen such a determined winter before or since. That's where I got known for my wood working, and it's kind of funny how, now, you're learning it," he digressed. He set the drawer frame on the drying bench with half-a-dozen others we had made in the last few weeks.

"And the rest is history." I unscrewed the top of my water bottle.

Sawyer laughed. "Not even close. Dominick finished that addition in under three months. Now, mind you, that was before electricity was in these parts. Come spring, he brought her out there. Had the preacher and the families. He told her, 'I built you the castle you desired, now, marry me.'" Sawyer did a royal impersonation of Granddaddy. "She turned him down flat. Told him next time, he should ask first. Your grandfather got down on his knees, asked her, and then hollered for a little hunting hound. You probably don't know this about Mawve, but she was the best pheasant hunter in the area when she was a little girl."

I shook my head. Even though Granddaddy had bragged all the time about Maw-Payne's keen shooting and that's what attracted him to her, and not the pecan pie that Maw-Payne readily claimed.

I put the big chisel set away in the rolling red tool box. On the way back to the work table, I scratched my jaw, trying to figure out what Sawyer's story had to do with me.

Sawyer tapped the mallet on the table to get my attention. "You and Dominick aren't that much different. You're here, building the perfect kitchen for the girl you've loved forever and a day. She is as oblivious as most that the woodwork in the barn and that desk that sat in the office until we repaired the old one was yours, and the fact that you love her like the crops need the rain." Sawyer peered over the top of the glasses. "Pass me the stain."

I handed him the stain, and all the while, I could feel my ears burn in embarrassment.

We took turns dipping our cloth rags into the stain and rubbing the color along the flower details of the office desk.

With the desk done, I picked up the fine detail chisel and worked at the intricate leaf pattern upon the drawer fronts of the bedroom vanity.

We settled into a rhythm of scrapes and mallet. My mind was matted with feelings. The thoughts were too jumbled to focus on just one.

"Ya want my advice?" Sawyer was going to give it anyway. "Tell her. You've already lost how many years by not telling her. She's been a part of your life since you were ten. Haven't you wasted enough time waiting?"

Lexi had been the one there for me—the night that I just wanted it to stop. The pain. The self-blame. The weight of Anna's death had taken its final toll. She didn't say a word, just called Doc, got me patched up, moved me into Mistwood, and harped on me until I talked to someone. Not even Monica knew how close I had come to ending my life. It was a secret I had never asked her to keep, but Lexi had.

Without Sawyer, I'm not sure I would have made it three years sober, and I hated seeing my brother sliding into the same pit with the demons of despair and alcoholism. Those were two demons no one could step into the ring against in our stead.

I dug the V-gouge deeper into the panel than I had intended. I gently tossed the chisel on top of the table and reached for the air hose hanging above the table. In short bursts, I cleaned the wood shavings from the tools and put them away. The air compressor chugged to life, feeding the tank as I sprayed a heavy flow of air across the table top.

With the shop cleaned for the night, our projects drying along the table, and the scraps stacked along the short wall, I leaned against the shop and watched the storm light up the sky.

Sawyer handed me a root beer and settled across from me. "You gonna take a shower before you go? The missus bought some girly shampoo again. I think she's doing it on purpose."

Chapter 8

My truck dipped into a massive pothole, and I banged my knee on the dash. One of these days, I was going to be able to come down the driveway without bouncing all over the place.

The lights were off in the house, but the kitchen light above the sink glowed, like a beacon, bringing me home. I drove around back and parked beside Lexi's truck.

The rain had slacked, but the occasional crack of thunder spoke of it gathering strength. I didn't wait for it to unleash the torrent upon me.

The screen door caught in the wind, banging against the stone house. I snatched it back and locked it before turning and dropping my keys on the table. The solid front door closed against the invading storm's bite.

I stirred the coals in the fireplace, not bothering to add a log to the dying embers. The iron screen slid closed, and I replaced the decorative fireplace screen.

The wood stack next to the fireplace was full, and I smiled. Lexi didn't have to do that. I refilled the firewood holder every night, and when I cleaned out the fireplace.

I paused in front of her closed door. My hand hovered over the doorknob. I shook my head and walked into my room.

I touched the side table lamp, casting the room in a soft, yellow glow.

My boots *thumped* against the dresser, landing on top of the other two pair of boots. My jeans landed over the back of a chair, and my socks disappeared under the bed. My shirt tangled in my damp hair, before joining my jeans.

I scratched my back and wandered to the dresser. For the longest time, I stared at the pile of briefs, many with holes chewed in them from Shadow. I moved the clothes to the side and picked up the tiny box.

The black box rotated between my fingers. Sawyer's words bounced around in my head. The box sprung open and nestled inside was a ring: The ring I had bought before Dad died. The white gold reflected the yellow light, and the simple line of stones held their shine. I snapped the box shut. I put the box to my lips before shoving it back in the drawer.

Eight years was a long time to hold on to a dream. Maybe it was eight years too many.

A noise set me on alert.

The clack of Shadow's nails grated against Lexi's closed door. The handle *tinked* and jostled each time his paw connected. The door handle flopped twice before he nudged his nose in the cracked door. He pushed his head through and opened the door all the way.

He came to me. His nose pushed against my hand. He took a step and came back.

"Need to go out?"

He shook his head and nipped at my fingers.

Lexi's cries were soft and muffled and set my pulse to a pounding thump.

The nightlight in the hall cast enough light to see into her room. Her hair was matted and plastered to her face.

Shadow licked at her curled hand and whined softly.

I eased around her twin bed. The soft glow from my room made her room an odd mixture of shadows and greys.

She faced the window. Only her eyes and hair peeked out from the spotted 101 Dalmatian quilt twisted around her. She whimpered and burrowed deeper into the blanket.

The bed gave, as I sat on the edge. I whispered to her, told her it would be okay. And that I loved her. It was the only time I was brave enough to. I braced my hand against the damp sheets. She couldn't stay in here, not tonight.

"Lex."

Nightmares weren't common. She'd had them off and on since Ralph's twisted fantasy played out the year before.

I peeled the blanket from her and tossed it to the side.

Even in the pale light, her shirt was damp with sweat. She shook her head, curling deeper into a ball.

"I've got you, Lex." I picked her up and headed to my room.

Immediately she curled into me. She sighed, as she relaxed. Her breath tickled my throat. Her nose nuzzled along my jaw.

I sat her on the bed. "Hey sweetheart, easy now." I tried to tug her shirt over her head. "You can't stay in that wet shirt. Come on, help me here."

Languidly she eased her arms through the shirt and shivered, as the chilled air crossed her naked flesh.

I swallowed hard and snatched my shirt from the chair.

The shirt glided over her head, and with a little encouragement, I pulled her hands through the holes. I glided my hand around her neck, pulling her unraveling braid from inside the shirt.

She laid her head on my pillow and drifted back to sleep.

The bed dipped, as I climbed in beside her. I tucked a strand of hair behind my ear, and mirrored the same on her.

Her skin was flushed, but her breathing was stable.

I laid a kiss on the steady pulse in her neck and pulled her close.

With a soft smile, she turned toward me and cracked her eyelids. "I love you, Ren. I just wish I could tell you that." She snuggled deeper into the pillow and succumbed to sleep.

She'd be mine soon. I pulled her close, covered us with my blankets, and closed my eyes.

Just as I tried to drift off to sleep, Shadow peered over the side of the bed and whined. "Well come on, dog," I told him. With a jump, Shadow curled into a ball at the foot of the bed. Lexi wouldn't be too thrilled that I let that mutt in bed.

Chapter 9

Shadow stretched across the foot of my bed, leaving no room for me to turn over. Not that I wanted to.

My arm laid over Lexi's waist, keeping her back pressed firmly against me. I nuzzled her loose, strawberry-scented hair and the soft earthy scent that was all her.

It was hard to sleep after her declaration. Instead, I laid here, with her soft curves pressed alongside me. There was something almost primal coursing through me. I stopped myself from slipping my fingers under the hem of my old shirt she wore, drawing small circles along her skin, kissing her neck and along her collarbone. These thoughts were too dangerous to dwell on for my own good.

Unwilling to wake her, I watched the greys of the room fade to a warm blush, the storm of last night forgotten.

She turned toward me, rubbing her jaw along my beard and sighing with content.

"Glad to see you're awake." I swallowed hard and licked my dry lips. I rolled onto my back, stopping myself from cupping her jaw and kissing her.

She snuggled in the spot I vacated before dashing toward the bathroom.

Shadow looked between me and the closed bathroom door. He jumped from the bed onto the pile of dirty jeans and shirts near the door. With a doggish grin, he curled into a ball, hiding his nose beneath his tail.

I sat up in the bed and laid against the wall. I kicked the blanket to the foot of the bed and rested my arm over my bent knee.

The door opened, and Lexi walked into my room. Free from her usual braid, her hair was a shaggy mess. Her lips were swollen and her cheeks blushed, as her eyes devoured me.

I smirked at the obvious desire coursing through her. "Join me?" I patted the spot next to me.

The pulse in her neck throbbed, as she swallowed. She shifted in the doorway. Her breath hitched in her chest. She suckled on her bottom lip, pulling her teeth against it.

"It's already six-thirty. I've got chores to do. I'm surprised Monica isn't banging on the door since you missed breakfast."

She had a point. Breakfast on the Laughing P was precisely six every morning.

I grabbed my phone from the side table and dialed the house phone.

Two rings and Monica answered. The thundering noise of ranch hands gathered around the kitchen table flowed through the phone.

"Monica, I'm taking a sick day." I didn't wait to hear her complain and clicked the end button.

My phone skidded across the side table and stopped beside the touch lamp.

Turning my undivided attention to Lexi, I gazed upon the beauty of seeing her sleep-tousled hair, the way my shirt flowed over her breasts, caressed her curves, and clung to her hips.

"There. I'm all yours."

I watched her squirm in the doorway. Her eyes travelled over the room, trying to find a way out. Yet the blush of her cheeks and the smile slowly growing on her lush lips encouraged me.

The bed squeaked, as I rolled off it. I braced my hand against the doorframe.

Her eyes went wide, and her tongue darted out, covering her lips. She shivered when I said her name.

"I'll make breakfast." I whispered in her ear.

Her heart raced under my shirt—a steady pulse that beat under the thin fabric. With a nod, she bolted from my room and shut her bedroom door.

I chuckled. Before, I walked on eggshells, unsure of where we stood. After last night's sleepy declaration, I knew what I was going to do today.

Shadow climbed onto the feed corn strapped to the back of Lexi's ATV.

I rechecked the shotgun and my sidearm and threw a leg over the foam seat. The ATVs rumbled to life, and we drove over the cattle gate heading across the fields.

Laughter echoed across the fields as Lexi and I chased each other over the familiar terrain. The ATV jostled and rocked under my hands as I pressed the throttle harder. My thumb rubbed against the rubber grip.

The game of cat-and-mouse had been played for years across our ranches, and I couldn't dream of anyone else I'd want to catch me. I slammed on brakes and skidded sideways across the rocky ground.

The engine revved as Lexi gunned it, taking the lead from me. She glanced over her shoulder. Her grin spread, as she laughed.

Not one to be out done, I took the lead, blew her a kiss, and turned down the path leading to the gazebo.

Live oaks refused to lose their leaves to the chilly weather unlike their white and red cousins.

I parked at the horse hitching post and turned the key.

Shadow jumped from Lexi's ATV. His nose hovered along the ground, and he set about investigating every scent and noise.

Lexi spun around on the seat. She folded her hands between her legs, keeping her fingers warm. She smiled as she looked over the pond and waterfall.

Squirrels overhead began chattering in frustration. An acorn bounced against the plastic fender, followed by another.

I dismounted and hefted the fifty-pound bag of cracked corn onto my shoulder.

The knee-high deer feeder sat under the spread of a cedar tree. The corn rattled against the metal screen, and bits and pieces fell through to the ground.

I wiped my hand against the tin roof, knocking off green sprays. I shook a branch from my shoe, and noticed, near the toe of my boot, a good-size hoof print dipped into the rich earth.

Strands of bark peeled from a sapling near the edge of the tree line. The pale white and green strings clashed with the dark browns and greys.

Lexi stood near the ATVs.

"I never get tired of seeing this place." I slid the shotgun from the scabbard.

"Neither do I. Grandpa always said this was Grandma and Dad's favorite place." She grabbed a two-way radio and slipped the clip onto her back pocket.

This place was beautiful. The waterfall crested the sheer rock, and the sunlight mixed with the clay, making the water gleam red. The waters lapped against the shoreline before following a small creek downstream.

Shadow bounded ahead, his nose parallel to the ground and his tail wagging back and forth.

Lexi and I leisurely strolled along the banks. She stepped upon the tops of slick rocks, and we tried to outdo each other on a game of spotting tracks.

The gazebo was beautiful. Thick rose canes snaked along the structure, and in warm weather, the chipped white paint was obscured by puffy old-world roses like the ones I carved into the desk and vanity.

I laid the shotgun against the railing. My hand checked my pocket, and I sighed, as I tried to calm the nerves dancing through me.

I offered her the bench seat and sat beside her. "You ever wonder the what-ifs?" I leaned back and looked around, trying to ease my growing anticipation.

"Sometimes." She shrugged.

"I wanted to ask you something." I shifted on the seat. My palms were damp, and I worried I wouldn't be able to hold onto the ring, much less say what I wanted to.

She turned to face me.

I pulled the ring out, refusing to lose eye contact with her. "I—"

The radio barked to life.

"Lexi. Darien. Either of you copy? Over?" Red's voice crackled through the serenity of this place.

"Lexi here. Whatcha need, Red?" She grimaced and mouthed, "Sorry."

My head thumped back against the support. So much for a perfect morning.

Chapter 10

Sawyer raised an eyebrow when I walked into his shop. He didn't say anything about seeing me at lunch time during the week, just nodded to Miss Thomas's side table.

I picked up the table and sat it on the workbench. The drawer stuck. Fumbling in the toolbox, I dug a screwdriver from among the hand tools, and unscrewed the bottom shelf. One by one, the legs joined the shelf and drawer.

I glided the sander over the leg. Sanding dust drifted in the air, and then floated in the sunlight. The leg landed with a *clack* against the table. Leg after leg, I sanded the painted wood down to the grain.

Sawyer's hammer and rhythmic hand sanding intermittently mixed with the whine of my sander.

I flipped the vacuum's switch and sucked up the dirt, while I tossed the worn sandpaper into the big trashcan. With the workbench cleared, I went to the massive shelving of stains and varnishes. "Do you remember what color Miss Thomas wanted?"

"It matches that piece we did last week. The walnut."

I retrieved the can and a clean rag from the basket. The leg of the chair rocked when I set the can down.

Sawyer set the sandpaper down and pushed up his glasses. "Okay. What's up with you?" He walked to the refrigerator. The light clicked on inside, and he pulled out two bottles of water.

I shook my head and shrugged. Nothing was wrong.

"Try again." He set the second water bottle on the table. "Start with what's in your pocket."

I glanced down. My hand was jammed into my jeans pocket. My fingers twirled the thin metal.

"It's nothing, Sawyer."

His concerned look forced me to continue.

I removed the ring and handed it to him. "I bought that when I was in high school. Dad took me to the city. I'd messed up with a girl, and I wanted to show her I was serious about her. About us. But, um—" I ran my hand through my hair, tossing the end across my shoulders. "My dad died not long after that."

"Lexi. I remember you two were an item. Dominick never told me what happened." He dropped the ring in my palm.

My fingers clutched the ring, and all the anticipation of the morning flooded me. "I was going to ask her this morning, but the sheriff needed something."

Sawyer scoffed. "That lazy ass—"

The shop phone rang, and he turned toward it and answered.

I ran my thumb along the flat side. Over the rim of the ring, the unfinished kitchen cabinets sat in the shop corner. Some of the cabinets were stained, but the upper cabinets were still naked wood. Picking a color scheme for the kitchen was harder than I had thought it would be.

"Bad news. The countertop won't be here until Christmas Eve." The phone *clacked* in the wall receiver.

"What's the excuse this time? Never mind, I don't need to know."

I shoved the ring in my pocket. I jammed the edge of a screwdriver into the stain can's lid and pried. The lid flipped and rolled on the rim, before it fell against the table top.

First, the door hinges were the wrong ones. Then, the drawer pulls were a mixed batch, and the colors didn't match. Now the countertop was delayed again.

I had planned on redoing the kitchen while Lexi went on her annual hunting trip, but everything kept getting in the way.

The wood grain hungrily soaked up the stain, and the wood transformed under my furious rubbing.

I laid the finished leg beside the others on the holder on the drying wall. It never failed to happen each time I walked into Sawyer's shop; I lost time while working on Miss Thomas's table,

My gaze travelled back to the cabinets. The lower cabinets looked better than the picture in my head had thought, but the upper cabinets needed something to pop. An idea pulsed under the surface, but I couldn't quite grasp it.

"Same time the day after?" Sawyer asked.

"Yeah, I think. Tomorrow's the actual solstice—" not to be confused with the calendar solstice. "I'm not sure what Monica has planned." I took the final sip of my water and tossed the bottle into the recycling bin. I checked the wood shop one more time before I pulled the heavy door closed.

"You gonna take a shower?" Sawyer asked as we moved toward his house.

"Do you even have to ask?" I laughed. I'd taken a shower every time I was here for the last three years—tonight would be no different.

Sawyer paused at the screen door but, before he could say anything, my cellphone rang. I reached in my back pocket and pulled the thing out.

"Yeah?" I asked as I flipped it open.

"Darien? It's Bubba down at the bar. I've got one of yours here. He's gonna need a ride, and soon."

I could barely make out what was said over the noise from Bubba's end. There was no mistaking the jukebox that blared in the background as any place but Bubba's place.

"Yeah, I'll be right there. Just hold them there if ya can." I looked to Sawyer and shrugged. "I got to go get one of the boys."

"Sure. I'll see you tomorrow at the party. You be careful." Sawyer and I shook hands before I walked around the house to my truck.

Chapter 11

The bar wasn't far down Main Street, just outside the city limits. It wasn't the town favorite, but it was the place to go to be left alone.

I pulled into the rutted dirt parking lot and circled the short rows twice before I pulled along the dumpster.

The pale-yellow bulb flickered under the short black awning above the door. Painted over the entrance was a faded billiard cue. Only the white patch around the number and a chipped painted circle against the black concrete blocks remained.

A group of people hung out around the door. Despite the cool weather, some of the women wore skirts just long enough to cover their thongs and not much else. Eyes followed my every move when I stepped from the truck and walked toward the door.

"Darien." The large bald man dressed in a leather jacket nodded.

"How you doing, Steve?" I asked him.

He was a burly man and not one I wanted to mess with on a great day.

"Same old. Same old. You know Trixie?" He wrapped his arm around the purple-haired girl.

She looked like jail-bait.

"Trixie." I nodded to her. It would be rude to ignore her now.

"Trixie, this is Darien. If any of the Laughing P boys gets in shit, you call him or Lexi." Steve's thick arm laid on the girl's shoulders. He pulled the girl closer to him. His hand roamed down the collar of her shirt. With a grin, he nodded to the door.

"Thanks." I nodded to the other guys as I pulled open the door.

The smell of stale cigarettes and peanuts smacked me in the face. I looked across the dim room. Small lights hung over the billiard tables and the neon signs made up the rest of the light. Some signs flashed red and blue and spinners twirled, all pointing to the bar.

I elbowed my way to the bar. Didn't everyone have enough stuff to do during the week? I put my hands against the top and leaned over the bar. Where was Bubba? Normally Lexi would be here with me.

"Just a second. Hold your horses." Bubba's voice rang out. I turned to watch his shiny bald head part the crowd as he came from the john. Despite his years in the Army, he was as round as his head was bald. He waddled behind the bar and pulled a couple of cold ones from the chiller.

Another patron held up his empty shot glass, and Bubba gave him a once over. "You had enough. Now get before I call your wife." Bubba waved the guy from the bar and turned to me.

"Darien. Just the man I wanted to see. Your boy's at the end of the bar." He nodded toward the dart boards.

"What do I owe ya?" I reached for my wallet, but Bubba waved it off.

"Just get him outta here," Bubba said before he turned back to his customers.

With a nod, I weaved a path to the end. I stood for a moment and ran a hand across my beard. Not who I expected.

"Come on, Damien. Time to go home." I squeezed between him and the rest of the bar.

He raised a glass and tried to take a drink. "Where my drink go?" He turned the cup upside down. A single drop dripped onto the sticky countertop.

"You drank it. Where's your sponsor?" I had to holler to be heard over the drunken rendition of some song. If I could have even heard the music, I might have had an idea as to what the guys belted out.

"It don't matter. No matter what you want. Poof. It goes." Damien spread his fingers out wide as he said poof.

"Come on, Damien. We can talk about it when we get you in the truck." I had thought Damien was doing well.

He'd gotten his thirty-day chip not that long ago.

"Where's your truck?"

"I don't know. It liked this beetle." He propped his head on the palm of his hand, and rested his elbow on the bar and grinned. "At least trucks don't leave you. They always stay the same."

"It's okay. We'll get it tomorrow." I uncurled Damien's fingers from around the shot glass and handed it to Bubba. "Come on." I tapped my brother's shoulder and moved from the bar.

"I like it here. No one cares. I don't wanna go." Damien leaned his head down on his arms and turned to face the wall.

"Damien. Come on, now. You were doing good. Let's go someplace we can talk. Okay?" I didn't want to carry him out of here.

"No. You always get what you want." He stuck his tongue out at me and turned back around.

What was he? A two-year-old?

"Okay. Have it your way. Make a hole," I shouted. The line was repeated and the crowd parted. I spun Damien around and hefted him over my shoulders. With a grim smile, I passed everyone and headed out the door.

"See you found him." Steve held the door open, as I squeezed through.

I tried not to bang Damien's head on the door, but accidents happen. "Yeah. You wouldn't happen to know where he parked. Would you?" If anyone knew, Steve would.

"Yeah. Don't worry about it. I'll drop it off in a few hours. You want it at your place or Maw-Payne's place?" Steve asked. Trixie held out a bottle of booze and grinned like a cat.

"We've got to come to town tomorrow." I wasn't sure how Damien would take to someone else driving his truck.

Steve raised an eyebrow with a smirk.

"You can leave it at Maw-Payne's." I shifted my brother's weight over my shoulders.

With a nod, I walked around to my truck and tossed Damien into the passenger seat.

The road looked dark and forlorn, as I drove back to the Laughing P. Guilt ate at me, but for what?

I thought Damien had fallen asleep until his head thudded against the truck window. "You always get what you want," he muttered.

"What's that supposed to mean?" I risked a glance at him.

"You wanna know the shitty thing. The only reason I asked her out was because I heard you tell Granddaddy that you loved her." He belched and laughed.

"Look, Damien. That's in the past. If she didn't want to go out with you, she wouldn't have." I liked it better when he was silent.

"Nah, you don't get it. I'ma no better than Ralph. Pull over." It wouldn't have mattered if I had pulled over or not. He hunched over and puked on the floorboard.

The one smell I could never handle was puke, and now that's all I could smell. I gagged on the stench and furiously rolled down the window. I could taste it in my mouth. If things could get worse, I didn't see how. At least on the bright side, I didn't have carpet.

"Here." I reached under the seat and pulled out a rag.

Damien pushed it away and wiped his mouth on his arm. "You were always Dad and Granddaddy's favorite. I never could make them proud."

Where the hell did he get that notion? "Damien. Granddaddy was proud of you. You went and served in the Marines, for crying out loud. Dad was proud of you. Star quarterback in high school. You and Monica got straight A's." I didn't bother to mention his senior year when he skipped so much school he almost got pulled from the football team.

I'd always thought dad had been proud of Damien and not me. It wasn't until after he died, I figured out just because we were twins didn't mean we had to be alike. Dad was proud of all of us.

In the dark, I wiped the lone tear. Some days I missed them more than I could imagine, and other days they never crossed my mind.

The rest of the ride went silent. My hands flexed around the steering wheel as my mind was a jumbled mess of questions. Would he even be honest if I asked him? With how drunk he was, would he remember tonight?

I pulled the gear shifter into park and peered at the darkened house. The only light on would be a nightlight in the kitchen. With a turn of the key, the truck quieted. The dash lights faded until only an afterimage was left in my mind.

The door squeaked, as I opened it and stepped into the cool night. In the dead of night, the only thing I could hear was the scrape of the wind against the pulley arm on the barn. The passenger door creaked open as Damien climbed out. He missed the step and crumbled to the ground.

I leaned over to help him up. He glared at me and pushed my hand away.

"I don't need your help. You've done enough." He staggered to his feet.

I tossed my hands up and walked toward the kitchen door. Whatever put his panties in a twist, he needed to dig them out of his ass before my foot joined them. Maw-Payne would hear about him at the bar by lunch time tomorrow, and it wouldn't do him any good as ranch manager either.

Buddy lay in front of the stove and lifted his head just to lick his lips before he crossed his paws and went back to sleep. The rest of the house was quiet.

Damien used the wall for support, as he staggered up the stairs and into his room. I fumbled around on the top of the dresser for the touch lamp. Its soft glow must have been bright for him for he shielded his eyes.

"You done your job. Go on home to the missus." His words slurred as he pulled off his boots and tossed them across the room into the closet. Well, he aimed for the closet.

"Can I call your sponsor?" It would be shitty of me to leave him like this. He was my brother, despite how much I wanted to strangle him lately.

"Dropped him like one of Monica's biscuits." Damien tried to pull his shirt off, but managed to get trapped in it. At least, that was one thing we could agree on. Monica's biscuits were harder than bricks.

"Stop." I knocked his stockinged feet over on the bed and sat down. "Stop feeling sorry for yourself. Why the hell did you go to the bar? I thought you were going to AA and had stopped drinking."

"You wouldn't understand." He laid down on the bed and covered his face with his arm.

"Look, Damien. I'm here. We were close before. Talk to me now."

The house settled. The furnace kicked on and warm air blew through the vents. The curtains on the window swayed slightly in the current. The overhead ceiling fan whined.

I thought he'd fallen asleep.

"She had wanted to break it off. I talked her out of it. I'd come home and sweettalk her. Laid down all the rules so I could keep her, but I didn't love her. I was afraid to. She didn't argue anything one time. That Christmas."

I didn't have to ask what Christmas. He'd quit coming home for Christmas after that.

"But, I love her as much as I don't want to. Now yer marrying her." Damien's choked sob rang in my ears. "I thought I had time to fix it."

I didn't know what to say to that. The saying about the path to hell crossed my mind. If I really wanted to make him feel better, I could have said, "I haven't asked her yet."

Chapter 12

In the front fields, many gathered in celebration of the true solstice marked by the longest night. The ceremony was over but the partying was in full swing.

The radio blared, and Monica danced with one of the twins. Her blonde hair looked red in the fire's glow.

"Hey, Darien." One of the Wundt's daughters tried to tease me as she dragged her hand over my shoulder.

"Hey. I need to get this to Lexi. It was good seeing you." I moved out of her and her claw-like sisters reach. Each time I'd ventured from Lexi's side, someone had decided that it was open market on "man meat", and apparently, I was top grade ribeye.

I took a deep breath and remembered I attended these things for Maw-Payne and that I couldn't go snarling at everyone.

Easing beside Lexi, I set a bottle of water next to her.

She smiled and nodded thanks while listening to Richie drone on.

"Did you see the video NASA released the other week? It shows the sun through different filters." Richie ran a hand through his dark hair and leaned against the bed of Red's truck.

"The rainbow one? That was cool seeing what parts glowed at what temperature and the wavelength correlation. The purple and gold were two of my favorites." Lexi crossed her arms and watched the people dancing.

Richie adjusted his duty belt, and his hand graced the butt of his service weapon. He fingered the polished brass of his officer's shield and leaned closer to Lexi.

I hadn't been able to add to the conversation since Red grabbed a couple of logs to feed the fire. I twirled a strand of grass and flicked it into the night.

Lexi shifted along the tailgate, picking at the bark. "I've got a few more pictures to take this evening." She lifted her camera and smiled. "But it was good seeing you again. Tell Lionel I said, hi," She nodded and departed toward Maw-Payne and Miss Thomas.

Richie and I talked about sports, but neither of us had common ground aside from the marked improvement of Tampa's team. With a nod, I wandered to one of the logs ringing the fire and sat.

The flames lapped along the logs and branches. Occasionally someone threw a prayer bag into the fire, and multicolored flames would mix with the orange and blue flames.

I pulled my prayer bag from my pocket. The small linen bag smelled of lavender and citrus. I hefted it in my hand and tried to clear my mind. A shadow fell over me.

Damien cut between me and the fire, spitting on the ground. He scowled, and I flipped him the bird.

I didn't want to deal with him tonight. The stench of last night still lingered in my truck, and his disregard for our family's traditions was just another link in the chain I wanted to hang him with.

At least Lexi stopped trying to talk to him. I knew she felt bad for how things ended, but she needed to stop punishing herself for other's actions.

Thinking of Lexi, I scanned for her.

She kneeled in front of Shadow. Her hands were buried deep into the mane of fur around his neck. He licked her face, and she scrunched her eyes and laughed.

Tomorrow, Lexi would leave on her hunting trip, and instead of a week of work to redo the kitchen, we were held up because of a lapsed countertop. I rubbed the bridge of my nose and sighed.

Jason's deep laughter drew my gaze. He sat on an ATV and flirted with a pretty brunette. He held her hands in his, kissing her inner wrist before laughing at what she said. With practiced ease, he tucked a strand of hair behind her ear and kissed her cheek.

I picked a twig from the ground and started to trace lines in the dirt. It snapped, and I tossed the entire thing into the flames. My face itched beneath the beard from the heat that flared up as Red messed with the burning logs.

I watched Lexi walk from the ring of light, toward her truck to leave. Shadow stopped and turned. He looked for me to follow. She paused and turned. "Come on, Shadow." Among the voices, I could hear hers like she stood next to me.

"You aren't gonna follow?" Red settled in on the log next to me. The skin under his eyes sagged and there was a weariness to him as his shoulders slumped.

It would have been so easy to follow. Slide in behind the steering wheel and take her home. That would have been the easy part. The struggle to avoid taking her in my arms and kissing her would have been the hard part.

But at the same time, doubt wormed its way to my core.

I'd watched Richie chat with Lexi on so many subjects, and all I could do was nod along unless it was sports, cars, or ranch-related.

Maybe I wasn't man enough for her. I'd tried to go to college, but even for a short time, the city felt more like a prison. I couldn't stand the towering buildings, people always around, and never true peace. She deserved someone who was just as smart as she was. Not some cowboy who couldn't pass high school without her help.

Red didn't say anything, as he set his jaw in his hand and perched his elbows on his knees. The fire crackled, and his red hair gleamed in the light. He scratched his arm and coughed into his sleeve.

"I hate being at parties when she isn't here, ya' know?"

Red tapped a cigarette out of his pack and tossed the empty pack into the flames. The little box curled in on itself before the edges turned brown and black. Within seconds the box was no more, and the flame moved onto the next. Right next to it was my little twig that a small flame tried to consume, but the twig laid there and let it. When it finally burned up, the flame went out too.

"Good love—true love takes effort. Something I didn't learn until I saw Chatan and Pam. After their son died, I didn't know if they would survive that, but they rallied together and shone brighter as they came to a decision. They had to believe in love to raise Lexi. It's hard holding onto the hurt and fear and raising a child who's just as lost but needs all the love in the world. There are days I miss them and Granddaddy. I'm thankful that I at least got to have time with them, and it was an honest relationship. That's all we can give of ourselves, our honesty and our love." The last of Red's cigarette turned to grey ash as he flicked the butt into the fire.

I didn't say anything but squeezed his shoulder, as I passed him on the way to my truck.

The drive to the Mistwood homestead wasn't far, but occasionally, it felt like it was a marathon. My truck rocked over the uneven Laughing P drive. The moon light was faint, but even so, dark shapes lurked in the field. Some moved and others stayed frozen in place. I kept my eyes peeled to the runoff ditch for glowing eyes.

I clung to one side of the driveway to avoid the giant holes that plagued the other. Back and forth I jostled down the path. The long-armed branches overhead twisted amongst themselves and barred even the stars from view.

The house was dark when I parked. Did Lexi already go to sleep? I slammed the truck door to get it to shut right. The sound echoed through the confined yard. If no one knew I was here, they did now.

I turned the knob on the front door and shook my head. Even after everything, Lexi still didn't lock the door. I couldn't blame her, since no one really did around here.

The television cable box cast its blue light on Shadow, who sat on the other side of the door. His tail swished back and forth in greeting. I knelt and scratched his head. If he was out, then Lexi's door was open.

I paused outside Lexi's door. Her back was to me, and she didn't stir at my footsteps. A part of me had hoped she would still be up, but Lexi never was a night owl, even on cattle drives.

Shadow pushed past me and settled in on the rug on the floor. He curled up into a ball with his nose under his tail.

I tossed and turned in bed. Even after a shower, I could still smell the heavy perfumes and unwelcome touches from the women at the ranch celebrating the solstice. I knew it was in my head, but it smelled real.

What I really wanted to do was lay in bed with Lexi. I'd lain beside her so many nights, with and without her knowledge that it was done. It's what I wanted.

I smashed my pillow again and threw my head back on it. As I tossed and turned, the blanket fell off the end of the bed. "Damn it," I grumbled as I got up again. It wouldn't be so bad if I wasn't freezing cold one moment and body burning with need the next. Wouldn't be the first night, but cold showers didn't help anymore.

I stoked the fire in the fireplace and sat on the couch.

The countertop was delayed. I wanted the kitchen finished, not halfway done when she saw it for the first time. I had built pieces for the office and the tiny bathroom too.

Maybe I could have Lexi delay it a few days? I disregarded that as soon as it crossed my mind. Lexi never missed the city's holiday party on the calendar solstice and Christmas.

My hair fell in front of my face. Shaking my head, my hair tangled with my beard, blocking my view. I dragged my fingers along my scalp, moving the unruly locks from my face.

Shadow padded from Lexi's room and sat on my foot.

I scratched his ear.

He licked my fingers and pushed his fat head under my hand, wanting to be petted.

The irritating bird clock sounded as the light sensor picked up the light from the fire. I rolled my eyes at the stupid clock. Maw-Payne was fond of hers, but the constant *clack*, *caw*, or *crow* had annoyed me since Dad had given it to her for Mother's Day. And the stupid thing had followed me here.

Midnight.

I looked at Shadow, his ears flopping back and forth under my hand. "You think I could go with her?" I couldn't believe I stooped to asking the *beast of clothing*.

Chapter 13

I stretched, and my fingertips grazed the popcorn ceiling in the living room. I walked into the kitchen and flipped the orange switch. The coffee pot began to gurgle and the rich scent of brewed coffee began to fill the room. Not waiting for the entire pot, I exchanged the glass pot for my lucky coffee cup—lucky because it was the only survivor after the tree crashed through the back of the house a few weeks ago.

Red raised an eyebrow.

"Morning." I held up the coffee pot.

"Thanks." He smiled and pulled an empty cup from the drainer. He dumped a couple of spoonfuls of sugar into the cup and stirred while he poured coffee into it. The spoon *tinked* against the sides.

We stood there, drinking coffee and listening to the house wake. The pipes in the walls shook, and Shadow padded down the hallway to the bathroom.

"I hope I didn't interrupt anything." Red blew across his cup before taking a sip.

"Nothing."

During the night, Lexi awoke and came into the living room.

Wrestling with the urge to lay her on the couch and kiss her until she submitted or chase her away for my own sanity, I told her about the one thing I hadn't ever told anyone but Sawyer.

I hadn't been in love with Anna. I had given it a good shot, but Lexi's laugh lingered in my mind. Her honey-toned skin clashed with Anna's paleness. Her gaze was always soft and welcoming, and Anna's had been piercing and determined.

It hadn't been fair for Anna to only have half of my attention and none of my heart. When I'd broken it off, she'd fled in anger.

Lexi didn't ask for more. She didn't mumble awkward sentences. She climbed into my lap and wrapped her arms around me.

I had finally started to doze when Red opened the screen door, setting off Shadow in a hyperactive series of barks.

Red didn't say anything about it. He nodded and stroked his beard. "Countertop still delayed?"

"Yeah. I didn't finish the upper cabinets anyway. I'm going with her."

Red chuckled, and it transformed into a cough. "She's going to let you. How'd you pull that off?"

"We've got until she gets out of the shower to figure that part out." I smirked. I refilled my coffee cup, and took the moment to savor the one moment of sanity in my morning.

"Asking for a miracle." Red cocked his head. Out of habit, he pulled a pack of cigarettes from his pocket and knocked a smoke from the package. He set the filter between his lips, knowing he couldn't light it in the house.

The shower clicked off, and the rumbling pipes quieted.

"Have those pipes always been that loud?" Red poured himself another cup of coffee.

"You eventually tune them out." Unless of course the one person I wanted in the whole world was in there, then the pipes became the trumpets.

"Blame it on Maw-Payne."

"What?" I stared at the man, confused.

"Morning, Red." Lexi padded down the hallway. Her braid draped over her shoulder.

"Morning, Lexi. Sorry if I came over too early. I wanted to talk to you before you left."

As she poured a glass of tea, the red hairband in her hair taunted me. It swished back and forth across her shoulders, and I couldn't resist pulling it free.

I laughed, as the twist unraveled, leaving her damp hair hanging around her face and down her back.

She cast her gaze at me before picking up one of the numerous brushes we had laying around the house. Quickly, she brushed, braided, and for good measure wrapped her hair into a bun.

"To be honest, Maw-Payne and I would feel better if you took someone else with you this year." He settled on a barstool. His hands wrapped around his coffee cup.

"Red, I've gone hunting every year since I was sixteen, alone. It's just for a few days." Lexi crossed her arms and glared at both of us.

"Yeah, but the rustlers this year and all. Please. Either postpone it until after Monica's guests leave so one of us can go with you, or don't go. We've got enough cows and chickens that one year isn't going to matter." Red tossed the words around half-heartedly, but the stiffness in Lexi saw it only as a challenge.

"Red, I go for more than just the meat. It's the only time of the year I get to myself." Her eyes bore into Red's.

I yanked the pink scrunchie from around her hair and plucked the red hairband.

She turned those beautiful sea-green eyes at me.

"How about I'll go with you?" I wrapped my arms around her, pulling her back against me.

Chapter 14

My legs ached from hours of riding, but that was nothing compared to the stupid predicament I had volunteered myself into.

Two days.

I lasted two days before I caved.

I shoved the saddle blanket into a ball and flopped back down. Every time I closed my eyes I saw Lexi standing near the fireplace in the cabin. Clad only in jeans, the fire's light highlighting her skin, obscuring the tiny scars that dotted her back. The warm, sudsy rag gliding along her arms and collarbone, and when she dipped the cloth into the pot, the lines of her full breasts made it hard to stay away.

I should have stayed outside the cabin.

Instead, I plucked the cloth from her hands, tracing the curve of her shoulder blade, and…

I turned away from the wall. The fire crackled, and shadows danced on the opposite wall.

Lexi laid on her back. Her arm above her head, an odd position for her. A low, throaty moan punctuated the stillness of the cabin, and my breath hitched. Lexi whimpered, and I shifted the growing problem in my pants.

She turned her head. A soft smile turned into an *O* as she moaned again.

I threw my blanket against the wall. The planks were rough under my feet, and I didn't bother retrieving my socks and boots.

In the fire's light, I watched her shift on the cot. My name tumbled from her lips, mixing with an all too familiar moan.

I should have kept walking out the door.

I sat on the edge of her bed and moved a strand of dark hair from Lexi's face.

She turned toward my hand, and I naturally cupped her cheek. "Ren," she sighed. Her tongue darted out, licking her lips.

My fingers trailed down her neck.

She moaned again. This time her head leaned back and arched at my touch.

I leaned over, softly kissing her lips. My thumb brushed over her nipple, bringing it to a bud beneath the layer of clothes.

Her low moan turned into a gasp that fueled her fast, shallow breaths. Her hand slipped beneath the covers, trailing down her collarbone and along her sternum before disappearing lower still.

I bolted from her bedside, tripping over my own feet and fighting with the chair as I fled out the door and into the cold night.

Stupid. Stupid. Stupid. I chided myself over and over.

I dragged my fingernails across my scalp, wrapping my fingers in my hair.

I ground my jaw, welcoming the pressure.

I hadn't come to take pleasures. No. The next time she laid under me, it would be as my wife not because I couldn't rein myself in.

This was easier before she moved back into Mistwood.

I tightened my fists. My breath condensed on the air and dissipated on the brisk winds.

The meadow was bathed in moonlight, accompanied by billions of stars. The horses snorted.

"Ren, you're going to catch your death. Come inside." She ran a hand over my shoulder blade down to my bicep. Her other hand curled around the bend of my elbow, and her warm breath blew across my arm.

"I just needed a moment." I swallowed the urge to tell her.

The final barriers between us had collapsed in the last two days, as secrets we had harbored for years—a lifetime—faded into just memories of the past.

My feet began to throb from the cold.

"What are you doing out here without wearing something other than a tee-shirt? You're going to freeze." I draped my arm around her, embracing her in my body heat.

The cabin was warmer than it had been when I walked outside, but the fire was little more than a pile of coals.

"Couldn't sleep?" Lexi held out the waterskin to me.

I knelt at the fireplace and stacked a couple of logs on top of the charred remains, stoking it into a happily destructive entity.

"Yeah. You could say that."

"I know the beds aren't big, but could I lay with you until I fall asleep?"

Chapter 15

On the last morning in the high country, I strapped the deer, rabbits, and squirrels across the pack horses, and double-checked the gear on Regan and Arwen. Too much weight, and the horses would tire before we made it back to the trailhead cabin.

Tomorrow we'd be leaving from the trailhead and heading back, just in time for the circus to begin with the town's party and Christmas.

"How much longer?" I tightened the straps on Regan before mounting.

"Three hours." She sighed, looking tired.

I might not be the greatest at telling time from the sun, but three hours and it would be too dark to ride.

"You okay?" I reined Regan in beside Arwen.

"Yeah. Let's get going and put some distance behind us." She tugged on J.D.'s lead line and led the way through the woods.

I hadn't minded getting a late start after spending last night with Lexi, but now that the weight of those actions loomed, I wished I had gotten us up when I awoke.

Back across familiar and foreign lands we rode toward the trailhead cabin.

As day lost the battle with night, the winds turned fierce. My fingers grew stiff through my riding gloves

The shadows beneath the trees stretched, and the horses slowed their pace, wary of things hidden in the darkness.

"How long until night?" I dismounted Regan, mimicking Lexi and Arwen.

She gazed through the branches and shifted to look at the red and orange sky. "An hour at most."

She pulled the lanterns from the pack horses, anchoring them to the rigging.

"You want me to lead?"

"Yeah. Regan's at least been ridden at night before. If we can get within a few miles, we can walk it, but the temperature's dropped steadily since lunch."

I couldn't argue with that. With the heavy coat, gloves, and thermal head gear, I still caught myself shivering.

She dug the Maglite from her saddlebags and handed it to me.

The weight of that light was more than just physical. Our making it to the cabin hinged on Regan trusting me, and me trusting her sure footing. One wrong move, and we could miss the cabin all together.

I saddled up, took a sip of water from the waterskin, and glanced among the glaring lanterns to Lexi.

She grabbed both pack horse's leads, and tightened her free hand among Arwen's reins.

I tapped Regan's sides, and we moved out.

Regan picked the way, her steps lost among the pine bedding.

The first round of howls set the hairs on my neck on end, and I instinctively tightened my thighs along the saddle.

Regan side stepped and snorted.

"Easy girl." I patted her neck, and the light jiggled against the oppressive darkness.

I hadn't meant to spook her, but while critters howling were common at home, none of the coyotes had ever sounded so close.

"Ren, I can't see to ride. Let's call it." Lexi hollered over the wind.

"Yeah. I can't make out anything other than the puddle of light. Should have gotten out earlier."

I saw her flinch and immediately regretted my words. Lexi made safety a priority and my own selfishness had endangered us. She tried to ease the tension trapped in her neck, rubbing her hand along her neck and shoulders.

With the reins divided between us, we began the final leg of the journey to the cabin on foot. The lights bounced with our movements, and things fluttered in the bush, fleeing from us.

The wind pushed against us and howled its discontent through the never-ending land.

"Lexi." I turned and she wasn't there.

I dropped the reins, unworried about Regan bolting, and rushed to Lexi. She leaned against a tree, mumbling about needing a minute.

"Lexi. Lexi." I tried to get her to stand. My blood pounded, and my adrenaline spiked.

"Come on Lexi. You need to get up." I tugged my gloves off and shoved my hand against her neck, feeling for a pulse. I cupped her face and pleaded with her to get up. Being trapped out here wasn't a place to pass out.

I scooped her up and whistled for Regan. Arwen stuck close and the pack horses followed. I laid Lexi across the saddle, and I steadied her with my hand. Regan treaded carefully. Lexi swayed in the saddle.

I don't know the steps I covered, or the miles, but luck was with me, as the moon shone on the trailhead cabin. Relief flooded me.

Lexi slid from the saddle and nestled in my arms like a sack of unruly grain. I fumbled with the door latch, and breathed a sigh of relief when the door opened.

I stumbled into the table and caught my foot against the leg of the cot. Blindly, I laid Lexi on the bed. I turned toward the fireplace. The place glowed in artificial lights and shadows, and I wondered why the damn light from the saddle packs hadn't pierced the darkness of the cabin when I needed it.

I pulled the box of matches from the mantel and struck it along the striker plate. The tip flared as the phosphorus ignited. Hurriedly, I touched the match to the handful of kindling in the fireplace and prayed for it to catch faster.

My hand trembled, and I realized I didn't breathe for the simple fear that it would snuff out the flame. The flames crept along the dried straw.

Time seemed impossibly slow.

In two steps, I was back at Lexi's side. I hurriedly stripped her jacket, revealing a sweat-soaked shirt. Her body was warm despite the chilly air, causing her flesh to prickle. Her shirt caught against her hair, and I yanked it free.

Her boots and jeans followed in her shirt's wake, landing in a pile upon the floor.

I pulled the fur from the back of the kitchen chair, shaking it out toward the fire to knock any unwanted critters from among the warm, dark hairs. Gently, I covered her.

The fear of hypothermia passed, easing the tension twisting in my shoulders. There were still dozens of reasons someone would pass out, and the weather didn't make that list any shorter.

I grabbed Regan's reins and led her into the lean-to, clicking my tongue for the others to follow. The first waterskin I grabbed from my saddle was empty, and my backup was nearly depleted too.

The waterskins on the pack horses were empty. "I'll water you guys as soon as I know Lexi's okay." I rubbed Arwen's white star and reached for the waterskins.

The weight of the pair surprised me, but the relief of knowing what was wrong with Lexi had me laughing. It was just like her to forget to drink when she was worried about a million other things.

I took the Maglite from my saddle. Within a few strides, I was beside her on the bed. I set the light on the floor, and shadows danced across the roof.

Gripping her hand was warm under the covers, I tried to move it into the light, and she tried to pull her hand back.

Holding her hand firm, I pinched the skin on top of her hand, and watched it bounce back. Dehydration slowed the skin's reaction. At least once a year, she blacked out from working too hard and not staying hydrated enough.

I held her waterskin between my knees. The plug *popped*, as I yanked the stopper out. I eased a hand around her neck, and gently pulled her up from the makeshift blanket pillow. "Drink for me." I winced as a dribble of water rolled across her cheek and onto the fur blankets surrounding her.

She licked her lips, and between her parted lips, water trickled in. Her mouth closed, and I watched her throat move, swallowing the meager offering.

I eased her down on the blankets, securing her among the pile.

Setting the waterskin on the table, I moved the two chairs closer to the fire and spread her clothes out on them before attending to the horses outside.

The horses snorted when the hand pump squeaked, and fresh water filled the trough. The game meat hung from pegs on the other side of the cabin. One by one, I stripped the gear from the horses, dragging the packs and saddles inside.

I stoked the fire and set a small skillet near the coals. Lexi swallowed a few more sips of water, and I returned to rub the horses down with a few handfuls of hay.

The hairless body of a squirrel laid on the table, and I was glad I had whacked the heads off the rodents. There was something disturbing about the furless bodies, beady eyes, and large teeth staring at me—following me.

I pulled the knife from my sheath and sliced the frozen meat from the bones, tossing it into the hot skillet. The smell of meat filled the cabin, and instead of fueling my hunger, it squashed it. I shove the pan to the side and turned to filling the waterskins.

The bed frame squeaked against the floor, as I sat along the edge. I let my fingers disappear beneath the furs, trying to deny the soft curve of her hip and the supple breast I stroked.

Despite the warm cabin, the covers were still cool to the touch.

Carefully, I picked up Lexi and the pile of furs. My knee banged against the floor when I laid my charge in front of the flames. I slipped her head into my lap and stroked the side of her hair. I repositioned the covers to hide the glimpses of naked flesh and silence the fantasies playing in my mind.

She began to stir, turning her face away from the fire. Her eyes fluttered opened, and her hands fought with the blanket wrapped around her.

"Easy, Lex." I grabbed the waterskin from the table and handed it to her.

She bolted upright. Her fingers clutched at the blanket, bringing it up to cover her exposed breast and sun-kissed flesh. A blush colored her cheeks, and she tried to hide behind her hair in embarrassment.

"You passed out. Your clothes were soaked, and you're dehydrated. I thought you had hypothermia." I gestured to her clothes I had laid out on the two chairs." My socks caught against the wooden floor. I picked up another blanket and laid it over her shoulders.

Greedily she began to drink the water, and I cleared my throat in warning.

Sheepishly she eased the stopper into the waterskin and handed it back.

I sat it down away from the fire's heat before joining her on the floor.

"How long?" She asked as she stretched out on the floor, wrapped in the blankets.

"Couple of hours." I guessed. I was fascinated watching her fingers glide through the fur of the blanket.

Her fingers crept toward my hand. "I'm sorry I scared you."

"You know me too well. Are you warm enough?" I diverted the conversation away from how scared I had been seeing her collapsed hours away from the nearest help; away from how scared I wasn't enough to save her.

"I'd like to be laying in a bed with you." Her eyes grew wide as she realized she'd said that aloud.

I chuckled, amazed at how we had been thinking the same thing. I hoisted her into my arms and stood. In two quick strides, I was next to the single bed and gently laid her down upon it.

I tended to the fire. Turning toward her, I stripped off my shirt, and enjoyed the ping of desire that lingered in her gaze as she watched it fall to the floor. Her tongue darted out as my jeans bunched around my ankles and I kicked them to the side.

Easing around her, with my back to the wall, I pulled her against my body, feeling her body mold to mine.

I wouldn't make love to her tonight, but that wouldn't stop me from teasing every cognitive thought from her mind.

Chapter 16

The sun had found us already on the road with the truck and horse trailer loaded. The horses occasionally stuck their muzzles through the trailer windows, and when we slowed to a crawl across the uneven road, they became a noisy lot.

Neither of us wanted to move from the single cot, but the drive loomed before us.

Lexi's head leaned against the window. Her eyes closed. How she could sleep with the constant rumbling over the uneven road, I'd never understand.

I fumbled for my phone, lost somewhere in the center console. It had stayed silent until we stopped for lunch, but now it vibrated, interfering with the music pulsing from the stereo.

Text messages flashed and a few missed calls. I thumbed through the list, most being the ranch hands cracking jokes and sending memes, leaving no doubt as to how they thought this trip would go. I paused on Sawyer's message.

I slammed my phone back into the console.

The countertop had arrived the day we left. *Give me a break.* That countertop was the bane of this remodel.

I plucked a brown hair trapped between my hand and the leather-wrapped steering wheel, dropping it on the floorboard.

I fed CD after CD to the radio. Lexi stirred, and without words, I passed her the waterskin.

She took a sip and drifted back to sleep.

I pulled an apple from the seat. The red flesh was firm, and the fruit was sweet. Within a few bites, nothing was left but the core. I cranked the lever, lowering the window, and chucked the core out the window.

Lexi woke to the cool air flooding the cab. She pulled my jacket over her shoulder and snuggled deeper into the seat.

"Looking forward to the party tonight?" She turned toward me, drawing her legs up on the seat.

"Same as last year." I muttered.

I hated going to these parties. There were three types of people: Those who didn't want to be there, the group that thought they were too good to mingle with the common town folk, and then the smaller group of people who actually enjoyed talking to friends and neighbors.

"Yeah. It does get repetitive." She adjusted the hairband in her hair and looked over her shoulder, gazing out the window.

I took a sip of water and offered her the container.

Our fingers brushed against each other, as she took the vessel. She sipped and tried to start another conversation. Silence was her usual preference, and I wondered if this chattiness was a result of her blunt reply to lay with me last night, after she discovered I had stripped off her clothes.

I kept running the odds of completing the renovation between tomorrow and Christmas Eve. Three days wasn't a lot of time, but with Sawyer and the ranch hands who had come in, it was possible ... maybe.

The sun reflected off the metal roof of the house and barn. I shifted in my seat. The heaviness of pulling off this surprise weighed more than I had expected.

Red waited at the gate, opening it for us to drive through. I pulled along the smokehouse near the summer kitchen and wasted no time unloading the carcasses.

Lexi began working on butchering. The hide from one critter landed in the stainless-steel sink.

Puffing on a cigarette, Red scratched one of the horses. "How was the trip?"

"Not the smartest move on my part." I gave him a cliff-note version of the last few days. "I need to convince Monica to do me a huge favor." I handed Red the last of the frozen bodies.

I pulled the truck and trailer around to the barn.

Climbing through the back door of the trailer, I unhooked the horses and led them to their stalls. The horses paid no mind to me I slung the blankets over their backs, securing the fabric with Velcro straps. The horses chowed down on oats and hay in their warm stalls.

Dragging the large hose from the side of the barn I climbed in the horse trailer and began to hose the dirt and shit out the back door. My boots sloshed through the runoff when I stepped from the back of the trailer. Turning, I angled the filth toward the large drain and let the rest run off into the grass.

"Red said you needed a favor?" Monica leaned against the barn door, away from the hose I held.

I flipped off the nozzle, and the water trickled and stopped.

Monica's hair was pinned up, and a tiny hat with a veil covered part of her face. She'd dressed nice for the Christmas party in town.

"Yes. I told Lexi you needed her to babysit." I wiped the back of my neck, sweaty hair clung to my hand.

"Maw-Payne already—"

"I told her you had a lawyer thing to attend to in the city. I just need you to occupy her until you guys come back Christmas Eve. The countertop came in, and I really want to get the kitchen done for her."

Monica cocked her hip. "And what do you want me to do for three days? Have you tried keeping her in the city? I can't promise I can keep her for three days."

I dropped the hose and dug in my back pocket, retrieving my wallet. Hidden behind my driver's license, I removed a credit card. "Shopping trip. My treat."

"Now you're talking my language. Why'd you lie to her anyway?" She grinned, as she plucked the card from my fingers.

"Cause I figured I'd at least get the office and bathroom fixed. I didn't expect the countertop to be in. And Maw-Payne and Miss

Thomas are going to need some time to plan something." I grinned as the tables turned.

"Plan what?" Curiosity curled her bright red lips, and she took a step forward in the mud.

"If I told you, it wouldn't be a surprise." I winked before turning back to the task of hosing out the horse trailer.

Chapter 17

I tried to remember the line about entropy and chaos. A too perfect world would collapse without some mayhem. Mayhem was all this job had been since yesterday. A leaky pipe destroyed the bathroom drywall overnight. And while the kitchen had patched up great after we removed the cabinets, the new cabinets wouldn't go in last night.

In the early light of a new day, we still couldn't get the corner base cabinet to go in. I slammed my hands against the front of it and stalked outside.

I didn't know if it was the tension of the renovation or the nerves of tomorrow, but I was irritated with myself.

Sawyer pulled up in his truck and limped up to the house. He paused at the door and rubbed his knee.

"Bad night?" He asked.

"If something's going wrong, it's going to happen on a schedule. What about you?" I nodded to his knee.

"Phantom pains. My knee hurts, but I don't have a knee." He chuckled the last part. His missing leg hadn't stopped him from being a damn good woodworker for the last forty years.

"Maybe you can figure it out. I can't get the corner cabinet in." I rubbed my hand against my forehead and sighed.

With a nod, Sawyer went in the house.

I looked at the yard—anything to distract me from the mess we had behind me. I hoped fairy tales didn't lie about grand gestures. It was nerveracking enough, and we weren't even close. At least the bedroom was going smoothly.

The screen door slammed behind me as I walked back in. I kept expecting Shadow but he was with Maw-Payne.

Sawyer sat on a barstool in the living room. "Did you try putting that cabinet in the other corner?"

As I looked at the corner cabinets, I muttered, "I'm such an idiot." We had put in the cabinets that made up the bar as a guide, and while the corner cabinets would work if we had placed them first and built from them, I had built the two corner cabinets to accommodate Lexi's backwardness. Lexi was a lefty, and most kitchens were set up with right handed people in mind.

"No, Sawyer. I was so focused on putting a corner in, I hadn't even considered that was the wrong one." I snatched a hairband off a hairbrush handle, and in a practiced move from years of too much hair, pulled it up in a bun on top of my head.

Jason's chuckle turned into a laugh that spread through the rest of us.

The kitchen came together like a jigsaw. Piece by piece, Jason, Sawyer, and I anchored the cabinets to the walls. Even half finished, pride in my craftsmanship swelled.

"I still can't believe you built these." Jason stood on the ladder with the level on top of the cabinet in front of him. It was heavier than it looked, and he took his time to screw the anchors in, much to the dismay of my arms and shoulders.

"It sort of fell in my lap." If Sawyer hadn't found me in the bar, I never would have given it a second thought, much less spent the better part of three years doing it.

The last cabinet up, Jason and Jeremy walked to the truck for paint supplies. I couldn't remember the last time the inside of the house saw so much attention. Every time I turned around, I bumped into someone.

The steady scrape of a trowel on drywall drew me down the hall. Had Damien shown up?

Red stood in the shower stall with a trowel in one hand and a hawk in the other. He whistled an old country western song, as he scraped some thin-set off the board and used the trowel to spread a thin coat.

I watched, as he laid the tile on the wall.

"Did you pick out the tile or did Lexi?" Red didn't even toss a glance over his shoulder as he spoke.

"Lexi did when we did the other bathroom. She wanted black slate floors and the sandy twelve by twelves for the shower stall." The little glass tile runner was my idea. Red wasn't that high up yet, but I hoped it looked as good as it did in my head.

Red's hawk was empty, so he laid it next to the open bucket. His jeans were splattered with grout and paint. Flecks of it clung in his beard. He wiped the back of his hand along his jaw before he reached into his shirt pocket for his cigarettes.

"Lexi would kill you if you lit up in here."

"I know. I'm heading out the door." Red mumbled something that I didn't catch over the string of cusses from the kitchen.

Red followed me down the short hallway.

Jason and Jeremy argued over who was painting and who was edging. Sawyer was under the sink cabinet hooking up the sink's pipes. It was just another reminder that hardware needed to be hung on the cabinets.

I walked outside and retrieved a Coke from the refrigerator plugged on the back deck. Red straddled a chair and the tip of his cigarette flared as he puffed on it.

"Where's your brother at?" Red glanced in my direction when I popped the tab on the can.

"I don't know. Probably with Alice." It's not like I had asked him to help, especially after the night in the bar.

"I doubt that." Sawyer pulled a water bottle out of the refrigerator. "He was at the dive bar the other night, sporting a new black eye courtesy of Lexi.

"What? When in hell does he find time to get in scuffs with her?" I could hear my voice get louder, as it bounced among the trees.

"The night you got back." Jeremy stepped up onto the porch.

"And no one bothered to tell me?"

"When has Lexi ever needed saving?" The trio chimed.

Despite the chuckle that turned my worry into a smile, I didn't mention Ralph.

A truck rambled around the bend in the drive followed by another. As the doors opened, the ranch hands who had been on vacation piled out.

"Someone called and said you finally got your ass in gear. What needs done?" Carlos asked, as he cinched his work belt. Behind him, the other hands did the same. On the short trailer was a new air conditioner and in the bed of the truck the new duct work.

It looked like the guys I called friends and family alike were going to make my dream a reality.

Chapter 18

The horses watched from the corral as we decorated the backyard at the Laughing P. The ladder wobbled under my weight. I yanked the burned-out lightbulb from the string of lights and shoved it in my pocket. The replacement bulb didn't want to go in, and with a little more force, I thought the plastic end would slide home. The fragile bulb broke between my fingers.

"How's the lights coming?" Red asked. He took a bandana out of his pocket and wiped his face. He coughed into the rag and scrunched it into a ball before shoving it into his pockets.

Despite the grey covered skies and chilly temperatures, we were all covered in a sheen of sweat.

I yanked my flannel shirt away from my chest and rolled my shoulders. "As long as no one shows up in the next hour, we'll be done. I think."

Instead of wrapped in warm blankets, eating sugar cookies, and playing with toys, Christmas morning found us stringing up lights and decorating for the party this afternoon. I laid a calloused hand on the thick branch and looked across the yard.

Lights hung between the trees and the buildings. Tinsel and garlands clung to the picnic tables, and the buffet table was coming together. The wind snatched a tablecloth off a table, and it danced across the yard, looking more like the Purple People Eater.

Maw-Payne ambled across the yard. She walked hunched, and each step her smile turned to a grimace.

I skipped the last few steps off the ladder and dropped to the ground. "Hey Maw-Payne." I greeted her with a kiss on her cheek. She smelled like mints and cookies, and my mouth watered at the thought of decorated snowmen and candy canes.

She looked at the sky and slowly blinked. "If it keeps up, it might just be a beautiful day."

I looked at her in confusion, but she shook her head.

"Monica and I are going to Lexi's. You guys need to start getting ready. Make sure you wash your fingernails. You still got paint from yesterday under them."

I looked at my nails and didn't see paint. What I did see was a busted thumbnail with a giant black spot under it. I couldn't remember which hammer hit caused it. They weren't the prettiest hands, but I worked hard to earn every cut, callus, and bruise on them.

"Yes, ma'am. Anything else?" I asked for good measure.

"Yes dear. Move the arch under the tree over there. It'll look better." She squeezed my hand before she walked to Monica's SUV.

Chapter 19

My breath came short and fast as I looked out the window. I tugged on the collar of my shirt. Without the tie, the shirt still suffocated me. Butterflies—they should be renamed velociraptors—swarmed in my stomach. I couldn't remember ever being this nervous. My tongue felt too big for my mouth, and I was parched.

We did this fancy party every year. It was a tradition. But the more I tried to convince myself, the more my heart raced.

A knock resounded on my door, and I turned from the window.

Rick carried Julie on his hip, jostling her with a bounce.

She giggled, and her chubby cheeks bloomed

"Monica still doesn't have a clue." Rick adjusted his grip on Julie's stuffed bunny before tickling her with bunny's kisses.

My head *thunked* against the window pane, tired of trying to give her space and yet wanting to swallow her in my embrace and never letting her go again. "How'd it go?"

He raised an eyebrow and let Julie down.

She held out her hands for the stuffed animal. She smiled when Rick handed the toy to her, and she tottered to the bed.

"You didn't ask?" Surprise widened his eyes.

I shook my head, unwilling to admit it had been incredibly hard not to call her, much less stay put at the Laughing P last night knowing she was home.

Rick laughed and smirked. "You better finish getting dressed."

I hefted the tie—it weighed more than a scrap of fabric should. I dropped it on the dresser and picked up the vest instead. The jacket glided off the back of the chair, and we descended the stairs.

Guests moved, talked, and danced to the music playing over the speakers, unaware of how important this entire moment was for me.

I watched Miss Thomas smile coyly at Nancy. They crossed hands and whispered before Nancy broke off to talk to one of the guys I went to school with.

The car door echoed, and I thought my stomach had dropped to my feet.

Jason jogged over, "They're coming through the house."

I could only nod, as my voice evaded me. My chest burned, and I had to remember to breathe.

The screen door opened as Jeremy led Maw-Payne out the door. Monica came next, and the door slammed shut.

Where was she? I dragged my nails across my scalp. All the fears I had fought for days flooded me. Did I plan all this for nothing?

Then the door squeaked open. My eyes widened, and my jaw dropped. I'd seen Lexi every which way, but she was radiant.

The dress was a dark green velvet with silver trims. It dipped lower than anything I had ever seen her wear in the front and the tops of her rich sun-kissed breasts peeked out.

As she took the first few steps, the skirt bottom swayed and I caught a glimpse of bare leg up to her thigh. I could handle the neckline, but that slit was almost too long for my comfort.

I looked back up. Her hair had been cut again, but this time it framed her face in layers, curling along her shoulders. I had never seen her wear it down on purpose, and even now, some of it was secured by a silver barrette that caught the light.

She paused at the steps and looked around. Uncertainty furrowed her brow.

I had to remember to walk—not run—to her. I thought sharing a bed with her on occasions had been hard to resist, but it was nothing compared to the desire that flooded my body.

"Ren." My name was a whisper on her lips. "You look good." The lack of makeup made the blush spread across her cheeks and up her ears.

"Thank you, m'lady." I bowed and offered her my hand. "That's a pretty dress." Damn, why didn't I tell her she looked pretty, beautiful, breath-taking, sexy, anything other than the damn dress?

"Maw-Payne made it for me. Do you think the slit's too long? I told Maw-Payne it was risqué." She moved to show the split, and my mind went to nights my hands had glided over her thighs.

If it was an inch longer, anyone would have known what color underwear she wore.

"No, it looks good on you." The grey trim matched the grey of my vest. I ran a finger along a piece of her hair. "You're wearing it down."

"Monica knows a really talented guy. He trimmed it up."

I put a finger to her soft lips and chuckled at her nervousness. "It looks good."

She let me lead her around the outskirts of the party. People danced and others ate, and we walked in a comfortable silence. Well, as comfortable as it could be when all I could think about was the ring in my pocket.

"Did you have fun with Monica?" I tried to ease the tension that locked my shoulders.

"Oh, yeah. It was fun." Her sweet voice fell just a note.

We paused under the oak tree. It was the first place I had run into Lexi, literally. It held many memories that I cherished and hoped she did too.

"Lex." I held the swing for her to sit.

She smoothed the back of her dress before she sat. Her heels crossed, and she put her hands in her lap. I wrapped a hand on the rope to keep from shaking. It felt as if all eyes were on us, but I didn't see anyone looking.

I knelt beside the swing and plucked a piece of dried grass from the ground. A snowflake landed on the sleeve of my tuxedo, a pale white contrast against the black fabric.

Just do it already.

I reached a hand out and twined Lexi's hand with mine. Her hand was small but it felt perfect in mine.

"In spite of everything, it's been a good year."

"Yeah, it has." I rubbed my thumb across the back of her hand, trying to muster courage.

"Hey, Ren, I want to tell you something."

Afraid whatever she said would make me lose my nerve, I interrupted her. "Don't worry about it today." I sighed, trying to ease the weight of anticipation from my heart. "Lex." I gazed into those sea-green eyes and cupped her cheek. "You're my best friend." I watched as her mind worked behind those beautiful eyes. "And life never seems to be on track." I fumbled in my pocket for the ring and pulled it out. "I love you."

Her eyes widened, and her lips parted on a gasp. She threw her arms around my neck before I had even slipped the ring on.

I buried my nose in her hair and inhaled lilacs and something richer—deeper.

She kissed me, tasting like she had all those nights ago under the willow tree.

I wrapped my hand in the hair at the nape of her neck and forgot where she began and I ended.

"Damn." I licked my lips. "I should have done that years ago."

As quick as the spark of desire had flared, it dimmed. "You're seeing someone." She eased back in the swing.

I cupped her face again, forcing her to look at me. "Lex, I haven't been with anyone since that night." I didn't have to spell it out for her as she pieced the woodworking and late nights together.

"But why did you move out?" Her eyes glistened with unshed tears in the soft light of the winter day.

I stole a simple kiss from her. Taking her hand in mine, I slipped the ring on her finger. "I've got one more question. Will you marry me?"

Her perfectly formed O turned into a smile. "I thought you'd never—"

"Today." I braced a knee on the ground. My fingers tugged on my shirt collar, and time froze for a single heartbeat.

Chapter 20

"You knew about this?" Monica crossed her arms, and tapped her foot. She sat across the table blocking my view of the dance floor and our friends turned wedding guests.

Rick chuckled and took a bite of cake. "Yep."

Lexi sat on my lap. The cord from the hand fasting twisted and pulled against my wrist as she shifted to nuzzle along my neck. Her warm breath rolled along my open collar, and my pulse jumped.

"Why didn't I know?" Monica lower lip jutted out as she pouted.

Rick offered her a bite of cake and a friendly smile.

She turned away from him, so he tried again. This time kissing her on the cheek and her neck.

She realized she smiled and tried to hide it behind a forced frown. She leaned in, taking the bite. Her eyes lit up as the flavors unfolded on her tongue.

Lexi laid a kiss in the hollow of my neck. "Because you can't keep a secret," she spoke to Monica while she nibbled on my earlobe.

The swarm of well wishes had died down, and for that I was grateful, but the fewer interruptions, the harder it was to keep from dragging Lexi into the barn, especially when she was purposefully tempting my resolve to wait until tonight.

Monica opened her mouth to protest, but Maw-Payne hobbled to our merry group at one of the picnic tables.

She kissed Monica on the cheek, ruffled Julie and Ethan's hair, and motioned for Lexi and me to join her.

We followed her onto the porch, and I held her rocker still as she sat.

"Sit. Join me." Maw-Payne nodded toward the vacant rockers.

I hesitated for a second before sitting in Granddaddy's chair.

Lexi smoothed the back of her dress.

My wrist bent uncomfortably, but the edge of my hand grazed across her ass, before she sat on my lap.

Buddy nosed his way out of the house, and the screen door slammed behind him. He passed between the rockers, wanting me to pet his floppy ears.

His short hair was dried and prickly to the touch. The diet of fish oils and eggs hadn't helped his greying coat.

He plopped down at Maw-Payne's feet.

Shadow bounded up the steps, tripping over his gangly legs. He sniffed the cord around our hands. He licked Maw-Payne's hand before joining Buddy.

"I always thought you'd end up with Damien, but Granddaddy knew differently. Even when you two were little things. He said Lexi calmed the wildness in you, Darien." Her voice trailed off, as she leaned backward in the rocker, and closed her eyes. "Where is your brother?"

Lexi looked at me with a mix of confusion and concern. She began scanning the crowds, looking for an answer.

"I'm not sure, Maw-Payne. I've not seen him since this morning." It was a lie, but she didn't need to worry about that today.

I pasted on a smile, knowing the disappointment in him not being here would pass. I traced the stain of Granddaddy's tobacco on the arm of the chair. Thoughts of Granddaddy and Dad filtered through. I wished they were here.

Lexi seemed lost in herself, missing family.

I cupped her cheek and waited for her to look at me. "I love you," I whispered in her ear, taking advantage to nuzzle her ear and lay a kiss on her neck. "How about we go home?"

She turned toward me, turning the tables on me. She peppered my neck in kisses, nuzzling the hollow of my neck. Her breath danced with her kisses, bringing my reined in passion to a simmer.

"You sure you can make it home? The hayloft's closer."

All of my reservations shattered with that simple remark.

I mumbled a goodbye to Maw-Payne, who smirked and waved us off.

Lexi smiled mischievously, and my heartbeat kicked into overdrive.

My palms grew sweaty. I dragged my free hand against the tuxedo's pants leg.

"Look at that boy go!" One of the Hardys hollered, and a few of the ranch hands wolf-whistled.

I flicked them the middle finger.

Lexi's laughter was the sweetest sound I could remember hearing, light and airy. It resonated with me like no other sound I had ever heard.

This was true happiness.

We eased around the partial open door. The sweet scent of fresh straw and saddle leather was mild in the winter weather. Our feet resounded on the concrete floor, as we moved quickly down the corridor past empty stalls.

I turned toward the hayloft stairs, but Lexi spun me toward the office door. Once inside the small room, she pushed the door shut with her foot and grinned.

I froze, caught in her devilish smile.

She lifted the hand fasting cord to her lips and pulled the knot apart, letting the multi-colored cord drop to our feet. Her eyes raked over me, and I squirmed at the obvious need dancing in her sea-green orbs.

Her tongue darted out, licking her beautiful lips.

I adjusted my pants and swallowed the hesitation.

Eight years of desires was a dangerous thing to turn loose on a wedding night—day. I wanted to last past a single caress.

She sat on the edge of the empty desk top, crossing her ankles. The green slit laid over her ankles, but exposed the rich caramel-colored calf that beckoned for me to appreciate what was higher.

I wrapped my hands in her hair, tilting her head back. Our lips met, and passion took over.

Her legs hooked me, drawing me toward her heat. Her arms snaked around my neck, pulling me tight against her.

My hands trailed down her side and over her waist, resting on her hip. My fingers curled against her, and she moaned.

I feared I'd shatter with each beat of my heart.

We parted for air, resting our foreheads against each other, but her nimble fingers didn't wait.

The comforting pressure of the waist band eased, as she unhooked the front clasp. The zipper resonated in the tiny room.

"What are you waiting for?" She nipped my lower lip.

Chapter 21

I bumped into the barn office's desk as I moved to give Lexi room.

She shook the velvet skirt of her dress and adjusted the cleavage. A smile hadn't left her face since this morning's surprise engagement, but there was a glow to her now.

She adjusted the pleats of my jacket, making it fall smooth along my neck.

I caught her hands in mine and kissed her. "Not what I had in mind for the first time."

"Who said we were done?" She winced when she took a step back. "I can't remember the last time I was sore," she chuckled and blushed.

"I didn't have time to make honeymoon reservations, but—"

"I'm happy just staying here with you." She tucked a piece of hair behind her ear. "Ren."

Just hearing my name on her lips was a slice of paradise. "We might be missed by now."

Her soft chuckle blossomed into a full-belly laugh. "I don't think they're worried. The Hardys did a good enough job announcing your intentions."

The office door squeaked open, and I tried to remember to oil the hinge tomorrow.

A *clatter* sounded overhead, and a squeal of womanly laughter mixed with a long, low moan followed.

We rose our eyebrows and smirked. Someone was getting some action in the hayloft. Not wanting to eavesdrop, we squeezed through the door and into the yard.

Music continued to play, and people crowded the dance area. A few smaller groups talked among the picnic tables, and Lexi steered us near Alice.

"Hey, Alice. Mr. Timothy. Did you try the cake yet?" Lexi sat on the end of the bench seat.

"Yeah. It was good." Alice didn't seem as upbeat as usual. She sighed and peered into her red Solo cup.

"Everything okay?" Lexi laid her hand over the redhead's.

"Fine." Alice didn't seem inclined to talk.

I was all for leaving her alone with whatever was bothering her, but Lexi wasn't that type of friend.

"Where's Damien? I hope he's taken you for a spin on the dance floor." Lexi tilted her head, trying to look at Alice's downturned face.

"That boy ain't good company lately." Mr. Timothy shook his head. His wrinkled hand grasped the cup, and it shook as he brought it to his lips.

"I haven't seen him in a few weeks. I hope that's okay—that I came anyway." Worry widened her eyes.

"You're always welcome here. Always." Lexi squeezed Alice's hand.

"When's the last time you saw him?" I thought Damien was just being a dick to me, but I also assumed he enjoyed Alice's company.

"He was at the dive bar a few nights ago. He was sporting a new black eye, but I didn't talk to him. I was doing a drop off for Doc Gables."

"That's the night we got back. I had a run-in with him." Lexi shrugged it off. "He's probably settled in with a bottle of Jack somewhere. I'm sure he'll turn up."

"I'm sure." Alice didn't sound as convinced.

An awkward silence descended, and we all looked around, trying to find something, anything, to talk about.

"I'm going to return the cord to Maw-Payne and see if she wants a piece of cake." Lexi hopped up and pulled the hand fasting cord from my pocket. With a kiss on my cheek she bounded across the yard.

I stroked my beard. *That was one way to get out of an awkward spot.* I smirked.

I nodded to Alice and Mr. Timothy and went around the picnic tables.

Jason and I paused to talk on the outskirts of the dance floor.

"How's it feel to be married?" He slipped his hands in his pants pockets and shifted his weight.

"Ask me later." Grinning, I winked at him. "Been pretty quiet." I nodded toward our friends and family mingling and partying.

"Yeah. It's different without Granddaddy."

I expected a sense of loss at the mention, but only joy filled me. Granddaddy would have been showcasing his newest carving or the funny toy he'd picked up. His talking fish sat on his dresser, surrounded by a dozen other gag toys.

Jeremy nearly knocked me over in his haste.

"Where's the fire, Hardy?" I turned to face the other brother.

"Um." He looked between me and the porch. "I need to find Monica and Doc." His face looked ashen, and his chest rapidly expanded and contracted.

"Doc's …" My words trailed off. "What's going on?"

"I don't know. Look there's Doc. Lexi needs him." He sprinted past me.

I turned to tell Jason to get Monica, but he'd already said it and was gone.

I sprinted up the porch steps and paused.

Lexi refused to look toward the guests. Her face was red, and tears trailed down her once blushing cheeks.

I looked to Maw-Payne, but there wasn't any doubt.

I kneeled beside her rocker.

A soft smile graced her face, and her fingers grasped a picture older than us.

Both dogs leaned against her knees and refused to move. Their dark eyes looked somber.

I heard Doc's uneven gait across the porch, but I refused to turn to look at him. If I looked away … this would be real.

"Monica's dealing with the guests. She doesn't know, like you asked." Jeremy's voice broke the bubble.

"Thank you, Jeremy. Ren, stay here. I'll go give our farewells." Iron control echoed with Lexi's words. No one would see her cry anymore. She would be the dutiful wife and ranch manager, and I couldn't even nod in agreement.

I tried to open my mouth to speak, but each time, my nose burned with unshed tears. If I spoke, it would be an anguishing cry.

"It happens. I'm surprised she lasted this long after Dominick died, to tell you the truth. She's with loved ones." Doc McGee walked to the edge of the porch. "Gables."

I tuned out the fuss.

Red's cough gave him away, as he joined the growing posse near the porch.

Rick didn't say anything, carrying the twins inside and away from the ruckus. The television in the living room clicked on, and sounds of Sesame Street filtered out the screen door.

The refrigerator door opened, and slammed shut.

"I need in there, Darien."

I glanced into the tired face of Doc and cringed when Monica's sobs tore through the air. Unable to stop myself, I turned away from Maw-Payne.

Monica's knees buckled, and she collapsed to the ground, holding her face in her hands.

Rick scooped her up, cradling her to his chest.

I stood, looking for Lexi among those who gathered.

All the guests were gone, except Miss Thomas's and Nancy's vehicles.

The grey sky spilled over. Snowflakes filled the air, and the rich green of Lexi's dress stood out among the white flecks.

She held the front of her dress bottom up off the ground, and headed toward the barn.

Ignoring the condolences of those gathered around, I slipped my jacket off and hurried after her.

Lexi spoke to someone in the open barn door. She shook her head, and her hair glided back and forth across her shoulders.

I settled the jacket over her shoulders and moved to stand beside her.

She tilted her head back and looked at me. "Thanks," she mouthed.

"I'm sorry to hear that." Miss Thomas smoothed her off-kiltered blouse. "She was a good woman."

"Yes. She'll be missed." Nancy adjusted her dress top. "You got a piece of hay caught in your hair." She reached up and pulled the golden straw from Miss Thomas's hair.

They stepped through the door and paused.

"We're sorry for your loss, Darien. You let us know if you need anything." Miss Thomas laid her hand on my arm, squeezing softly. She hesitated, as if she wanted to say something but didn't.

Nancy brushed past us and hurried to her car.

"They—they were the ones—" I looked over my shoulder at the couple.

Despite the sadness in Lexi's eyes, she smiled softly. "You didn't really believe Miss Thomas slept with the sheriff, the judge, and everyone else in town for gossip, did you?"

I draped my arm around her, pulling her close. "To tell you the truth, I never really thought about it."

Lexi didn't say anything.

There was nothing that could be said.

We had lost the Payne matriarch.

Chapter 22

Lexi squeezed my hand and nodded toward Doc.

I gave her a small smile in thanks and stepped forward.

Nothing was the same, yet it was. Routine became our comfort in the days after Maw-Payne died.

I traced the flowers on top of Maw-Payne's casket, adding mine to the pile. *I love you.* I silently nodded to the box and stood before those gathered.

Most eyes were glazed with unshed tears, fighting to maintain their dignity and strength for those gathered.

"Thank you for coming."

Rick had his arms full with the twins, who were unaware of the meaning of this goodbye, and Monica.

"Maw-Payne, Mawve—" it was weird saying her name, "was a friend, a mother, and a grandmother to everyone. She always had a spot open at the table for everyone." I cleared my throat, unsure of what to say next.

"And she will be missed, but her legacy will live on. We remember," Lexi spoke.

We remember rippled through the people, gaining volume as they chanted.

Lexi came forward and took my hand. She absentmindedly tossed her braid over her shoulder. "We remember and that is enough. We remember her kindness."

The crowd echoed, "We remember."

"We remember her wisdom." Lexi's voice gave no sign of quivering.

"We remember." The town echoed again.

"Maw-Payne will live on in our tales, and she will shine as the pillar of our community she was."

As one the town's voice rang through the cemetery, breaking my heart and yet taking the pain with it. We all suffered her loss, and here we stood, suffering and remembering together.

For a minute or two, those gathered stood around, not wanting to be first in the long, winding line of farewells.

Miss Thomas, dressed from head to toe in black, squared her shoulders and marched to the resting body. She kissed the tulip and laid it with the flowers. With a curt nod, she turned from the casket and raised her clutched tissues to her eyes, dabbing the gently falling tears.

Friends and neighbors offered their condolences. Monica nodded to them, in the same catatonic state she'd been for the last five days.

Rick switched sides, squeezing in between Lexi and Monica. The twins clung to him, each taking turns to tug on his tie and nuzzle his neck.

Lexi greeted everyone by name, shaking their hands and exchanging their impromptu hugs, despite her rarely being a hugger herself. She tried to laugh and smile, as the guests and she recounted memories and moments involving them and Maw-Payne.

That simple gesture brought a smile to my lips and to many of those gathered.

The ranch hands surrounded the casket. Laughs and sniffles punctuated their chatter.

"Mull." I acknowledged the sheriff.

I had never liked the man. Firefighters and cops were like football teams, community united us, but aside from that, we tossed minor insults at the other.

"Darien, can I talk to you for a moment, over there?" He tossed his head away from the group.

I sighed and extended my arm for him to go first.

Mull adjusted his belt, pulling it over the edge of his stomach. He grunted, as he shifted his weight.

"Have you seen Damien?"

I crossed my arms.

With how often Damien was coming up in conversations, I began to wonder if I'd be seeing his mug shot on America's Most Wanted.

"Not in a few days."

"I hate to do this, especially today, but Donna escaped custody." Mull scratched the sagging skin under his eye. "If you see or hear anything, can you call me?"

I scoffed. I wouldn't trust this man to direct traffic, much less catch a conniving bimbo.

Ethan screamed, and I looked toward the toddler commotion.

Lexi waited a beat to see if Monica responded before taking Julie. She gave Rick a sad smile.

Rick, tight-lipped, wrangled a stiff Monica and Ethan toward their SUV.

"Sure. I need to get back." I brushed past the man.

I pulled my truck alongside Lexi's and Red's. Ranch hands had parked haphazardly, and I was surprised Lexi hadn't made them park along the fence.

My boots thumped up the porch steps, and I hesitated at the vacant rocker of Maw-Payne's.

The wind blew around the edge of the house. A couple of the rockers began to sway to-and-fro, out of sync, and the scrapping of the runners against the porch boards calmed my nerves bundled in a knot.

There was so much to do, and while it wasn't a year ago we did the same things when Granddaddy died, this time it felt permanent.

"Simmer down. I know it's crowded." Lexi's voice carried over the commotion in the kitchen and out the screen door.

I braced an arm against the door, out of sight, and sighed. I wasn't sure I wanted to face the dozen or so people in the kitchen.

"Guys! I know it's crowded. Simmer down. Please. Darien and Monica have their hands full, so for the immediate future, any ranch problems come to me. I don't know what's going to happen as far as the Laughing P is concerned, and for now, we'll stick to routine. Now … what?" Lexi leaned against the sink, her ankles crossed.

"You don't think—" I couldn't see who asked, and over the shuffling of bodies, it sounded garbled.

"I don't know anything. Until the executor reads the will, I know as much as you do. Can I continue or are there more questions that I can answer with the same line?" she snapped, wrangling control from the high-strung emotions of the last few days. "I do not know what is going to happen. Until then, we run like we have."

"You don't mean one of those no-show children could end up with the ranch, do you?" Another ranch hand gruffly spoke.

I couldn't blame any of them for that fear. Maw-Payne and Granddaddy had seven children, five were still alive, and none of them had appeared at their funerals.

"Are we rotating who cooks and stuff?" Nathan, one of the guys from the mill, asked.

"Y'all ain't ate?" Lexi surveyed the room.

A chorus of whatever was in the bunkhouse and Lola's filled the room.

"I can't promise food at six, but expect breakfast before work. I'm not sure who is doing Maw-Payne's chores."

"I've done them the last few days," Red spoke up, "and Rick's tried doing Monica's."

Lexi pinched the bridge of her nose and sighed. "We'll work things out tomorrow." She sighed and crossed her arms. "Take today off. Go do something that isn't sitting in the bunkhouse."

Shadow raced through the kitchen, launching himself against the screen door. His nails caught against the porch. He turned his nose, leading his entire body, toward me. He licked my hand and followed me into the house.

The guys gave tight-lipped smiles and silent nods.

I kissed Lexi on the cheek and headed to the office.

I hadn't been in the office, in any official capacity, in a couple of months—not since Damien took over as ranch manager after he came home.

I righted Granddaddy's carved whale on a shelf of the floor-to-ceiling bookcase. Maybe I had been a spectator in the room since Granddaddy died, but the office had always been a mix of Dad and him. And I liked it like that.

The little differences made my stomach churn.

Damien had moved the shelf decorations around, hiding more than a piece or two in the bottom cabinet.

I sat in the chair. My eyes widened. In the recently refinished glossy coat, a two-inch long gash marred the desk.

"How …" I shook my head. I didn't want to know who, much less what, dug into the recently refinished desktop.

I slid the desktop calendar to the edge, obscuring the offending mark. The calendar was off a month, and doodles filled every blank space. I tore the page off until December gleamed. Maw-Payne's flowery cursive filled in the family days.

The New Year was a few days away. As far back as I could remember, we always had a bonfire, filling the night with firecrackers, bottle rockets, and music cranked way too loud.

I twirled the pen between my fingers before shoving it in the pen cup. I'd ask the guys later if anyone was interested in one.

Granddaddy had always kept the current year finances in the right pullout drawer and important documents along with blank printer paper in the left cabinet. When I opened it this time, disarray stared back at me. A bottle of liquor lay atop cream-colored file folders, bent nearly in half, which filled both cabinets.

I gave each folder a once over before stacking it on the desk. Finances ranged from years before the merger to supplies bought last week at the Feed and Seed, layered upon each other in a tangled mess of papers, folders, and receipts.

A heavy rap on the office door broke the mundane task. Rick poked his head in.

I nodded for him to come on in.

Julie stuck her head in the door before scampering down the hallway toward the catchy theme songs of cartoons.

The Grandfather clock chimed, and I blinked. Where had the afternoon gone?

"Can I ask you something?" Rick moved a crinkled paper ball from a chair and sat down.

"Yeah." I rubbed the back of my neck and stretched in the chair. The slow throb of being chained behind the desk began to blossom.

"When are you going home?"

"When things die down, I guess." I hadn't intended on crashing here the last few days, but between funneling phone calls and handling details of Maw-Payne's burial I hadn't planned on anything other than the next item on my to-do list.

"You're not helping Monica any. She won't snap out of this funk as long as everyone keeps doing everything for her. She needs a job to do. Are you going to be there next week after we pack up and move back here? You going to watch the kids while I meet with Mr. Ronald and Mr. Mull? You going to feed the men that need to know that they're still a part of this family?" He sighed.

I stared at him, his words playing through on repeat. "Wait. You're moving here? This wasn't because of Maw-Payne, was it?"

"No. I gave my notice before Christmas, and Lexi helped me set up interviews with the people here to see what I could possibly do." He stood and his fingers straightened the pencil holder on the edge of the desk. "You've been married less than a week, and you haven't even been home. Think on it."

Chapter 23

I walked in the door, setting my keys and hat on the side table. My jaw dropped, as I took in Lexi.

She kneeled near the refrigerator. Dog food poured from the green bag and into Shadow's bowl. A few brown bits bounced across the floor, and he chased after them.

She set the bag on top of the fridge and turned. The overhead light glinted off stud-earrings, and her hair, half up, teased for me to run my fingers through the soft curled locks.

I licked my lips and exhaled.

The sweater hung off her shoulder, hinting at soft curves. The new jeans had a crease running down the front. The dark fabric hugged her ass and thighs. The bottom of the jeans flared over grey knitted boots that I knew she didn't have before she went with Monica to the city.

"You're home." She seemed surprised to see me.

"You look good. Going somewhere?" I tried to remember if she had said something.

"The Barn. I reminded you this morning and sent a text." She didn't say anything else, but her shoulders dropped a little, and the sweater dipped lower on her shoulder.

"Yeah." I didn't remember the last time I ate, much less this morning's conversation. "Give me enough time to shower and change." My fingers trailed along her arms. The sweater caught against my callused fingers, and the little smile she gave me chased the tiredness from me.

The master bedroom looked undisturbed, not even a pair of dirty socks or forgotten pajamas lay in sight.

I pulled open a drawer and stared at emptiness. In the chaos of the last few days, I had forgotten to bring my clothes after the renovation.

Weighing the pros and cons, I plucked the front of my shirt out and sniffed the fabric. Lucky for me, I had changed from the funeral attire to jeans and a tee-shirt; it was going to have to work for tonight.

"You ready?" I walked into the kitchen.

Lexi scratched Shadow behind the ear before giving the pup a rawhide. "Be good," she whispered, as she kissed the tip of his black nose.

I stopped myself from smirking.

Shadow behave? The dog constantly destroyed my clothes and shoes, and not even the red or black Kongs for dogs kept the pup's attention. We had tried crating him, but he had learned to push his feet through the bars and move around the floor, and when that didn't appease him, he kicked the tray out, destroying the floor with his oversized paws.

She stood and gave me a once-over. Her eyebrow rose, but she shook her head, and grabbed her jacket from the wall-mounted coat rack.

I grabbed my hat and followed her.

We paused at the trucks. Did it matter whose truck we took now? No one ever mentioned these awkward moments when they talked about marriage.

"Here. Let me get the door for you." I walked to the passenger side of my truck.

She took a deep breath before climbing into the cab, reminding me that I needed to get the running boards replaced—a task two years on my to-do list.

I hurried around the back of the truck and slid into the driver's seat. I turned the volume down on the radio before cranking the truck. Outlaw Country poured from the speakers. I cringed and scrambled to turn down the radio volume some more.

Lexi stared out the window, her mind elsewhere.

The drive to The Barn was unusually quiet. Each of us asked questions, but the other seemed set on one-word replies.

I shifted in the seat and cranked open the window. The chilly bite of winter whistled through the opening, and parts of Lexi's hair ruffled in the breeze.

Absentmindedly, she tucked the strand behind her ear and continued to gaze into the darkness.

On the outskirts of town, The Barn stood brightly lit in the middle of the field. White lights hung from the doorway and across the pergola-covered patios.

I parked among the rows of vehicles. Before I could open Lexi's door, she had slid from the seat and was waiting for me at the tailgate.

Honky-tonk music began to pour from the speakers, spreading like ripples from inside the redone barn and into the parking lot.

We fell in step, and she slipped her hand into mine. I glanced down and smiled. Raising our hands, I kissed the back of her hand and winked at her.

Under the lights, a blush rose in her cheeks and colored her ears.

We passed town-folk, walking to and from the bar and exchanged nods in greeting. I caught the eyes of a couple of local jocks after they had taken more than enough time to appreciate Lexi. Their smiles and playful shoves turned to bashful glances, as they studied the grass under their tennis shoes.

Lexi's soft chuckle became lost as the music swallowed us.

Inside The Barn, a dance floor teemed with people and others sauntered around the perimeter, taking seats along the tables and bar chairs.

She squeezed my hand and led the way to a row of tables that overlooked the billiard tables.

Jason and Jeremy raised their beers in greeting, taking a sip afterwards.

"Thought you were on your way half an hour ago?" Jeremy ran a hand through his spiked hair.

"Shit happens." Lexi climbed onto the barstool. She leaned over and kissed me on the cheek.

I was captivated by her smile, as she leaned back in the chair. Her hair curled along the top of her sweater, acting like an arrow pointing to the lacy top of a bra peeking out from the sweater.

Curiosity coursed through me, as I wondered what other trinkets she had picked up on her shopping spree in the big city.

Rachael walked by, carrying a tray laden with beer bottles and mugs shoulder high. Without missing a step, she handed me two Cokes.

In the next beat, one of the rowdy guys a table over dragged his hand along her bare midriff. Rachael caught his hand and bent it back until he nearly fell out of the chair. "Don't touch the merchandise dick-weed." She spun in a perfect little circle and not a single drink wobbled.

"Are you allowed to stare like that now?" Jason joked.

I turned my attention back to the table. "What?"

Lexi's smile turned into a chuckle. "Forget it, boys. Can't stop nature." She rolled her eyes, and I caught a glimpse of her knitted boot swinging under the table to the beat of the music.

The music stopped, but the rustling of bodies drowned out the bar owner Kenny, as he stood at the microphone near the D.J.'s booth. Kenny tried to speak again, but the crowd's volume seemed to rise as they competed to hear themselves over their neighbors. He smirked and talked to the D.J. secured behind the plexiglass. He brought his fingers to his lips, and a piercing whistle tore through the sound system.

"Thank you. Now, many here gather to celebrate the life of Mawve. Many of you know the little old lady, and her infamous wooden spoon, as Maw-Payne."

A chorus of cheers and clinking glass resounded through the bar.

"In honor of her, let's kick it off with some dancing!" Kenny stepped away from the microphone.

The lights above the dance floor flashed the full rainbow. The first few beats of Alan Jackson set a round of applause through the crowd.

Lexi looked to me, and I took a sip of Coke.

"Come on." Jeremy and Jason grabbed Lexi's hands.

She shrugged and slid off the stool. Her sweater shifted along her collarbone and dipped off her shoulder.

They led her to the dance floor, and seamlessly the trio slipped into the line dance.

With each kick and turn, her smile grew until it was a permanent fixture with her flushed cheeks.

Jason was the first to bow out, as the song changed again. He plopped down in the seat across from me and drank the rest of his beer. "She is hell to keep up with," he panted between breaths.

I propped my elbow on the table, resting my jaw in my hand. "Blame it on the line dancing classes Maw-Payne dragged her and Monica to."

Each time she faced our way, her eyes locked with mine, and a force tugged at me to join her.

B-52's "Love Shack" filtered through the surround sound, and I smiled at all the memories I had of catching Maw-Payne dancing in the kitchen to the song.

The sea of people parted—men on one side and women on the other.

Lexi looked around the floor, and her smile fell a little. She hid her face behind a wall of hair and moved from the floor, circling the long way back to the table.

"Really?" Jeremy raised an eyebrow and leaned forward for another beer.

"What?" I looked between the brothers, thinking I missed something.

Jason shook his head and smirked. "Nothing." He grabbed a handful of peanuts, cracking the dried shells and tossing the empty husks onto the floor. His pyramid of red-skinned peanuts grew, and one or two rolled off the table.

I twisted in the seat, scanning the place for Lexi, but without her iconic braid, I couldn't pick her out in the flickering lights.

Jeremy's hand landed over Jason's pile, and in one swoop, picked every peanut up before shoving them into his mouth. He smirked, as he ate his brother's hard-earned bounty.

"Come on, bro. Those were mine." Jason pushed his brother, and Jeremy scrambled to stay on the stool.

"Can't you boys throw your empty bottles in the bin?" Lexi set the edge of a nacho platter on the table.

Immediately the pair picked up the empty bottles and tossed them into the giant trash bin near the wall.

She slid the rest of the platter onto the table and climbed onto the stool. She didn't say anything, as she stretched a cheese laden chip above the pile. Piece by piece, she flicked the tomatoes back onto the pile and broke the cheese free. Before she had finished devouring the chip, she was eyeballing her next conquest.

Jason and Jeremy reached for the container of peppers. Without saying a word, they nodded to each other and put a full pepper in their mouth. With each bite, their faces turned redder, and their brows glistened in sweat.

Lexi paused in mid bite. Her sea-green eyes tracked between the Hardys, waiting for one to give in to the heat.

I'm not sure who broke for the beer first. One instant, their faces were contorted, and the next, they were downing their beer.

"Did I forget to mention those weren't the usual peppers but Kenny's new cross-pollinated ones?" Her teeth tugged against her bottom lip, as she tried not to chuckle.

That simple little action made me wet my lips. Goosebumps covered my arms, and I tugged at the collar of my shirt.

"Can you hear me?" Kenny tapped on the microphone again. He looked over the crowd before he continued. "In honor of one of the greatest women we ever knew, let's have a dance off. Ten songs, grab your partner, and let's see you shake what you've got."

Lexi looked at me. Her lips parted, but she didn't speak. She shook her head and leaned her forearms against the table. Her fingers interlaced; the roving light glinted off her ring.

My hand instinctively went to my bare finger. Nothing to roll and twist around my fat finger.

"Come on." I grabbed her hand and led her from the table.

I hated dancing, but that wasn't because I couldn't.

Her hand twisted and pulled, as she tried to keep pace with my stride.

We claimed our piece of the floor, and I prepared for the worst possible song selection in the history of this place.

What was a competition if the first song wasn't "Achy Breaky Heart?"

I shook my head but gave into the crowd of people doing the same dance. There wasn't an excuse in the world that would suffice for not knowing a typical line dance—it was taught in P.E.

Songs older than me to modern favorites played, and couples and friends dropped from the dance floor, but not Lexi and me.

There was something so utterly freeing about pounding the ground with our steps and not giving a damn about tomorrow.

We leaned forward and back, kicking our heels before turning. Lexi glanced at me when we leaned forward again, and all I could see was the lacy bra framed by that soft sweater she wore.

I missed a step and turned a half beat too late.

"Enjoy the eyeful?" She laughed at my stumble but didn't miss a beat as the song changed to "Raise Up."

I tipped my hat to her and shifted the front of my jeans.

In our little corner, we moved to the music, embellishing the rhythmic moves with more style than Maw-Payne would have ever approved.

"Country Girl, Shake it for Me" pounded through The Barn, and most on the floor groaned as their energy faltered.

"I didn't know you were a Bryan fan." I had to shout for Lexi to hear me over the crowd.

"He's got good music, but I'm not smiling for that. This song always drops people from the floor." She brushed against me, as she turned to face the interior of the remaining group.

What had started as a full floor had indeed dwindled to just a dozen couples. By the end of each chorus another group began to misstep.

I lost track of the songs played, and my chest burned for oxygen. During the few seconds of interlude as the D.J. rambled about what was coming up soon, I stretched to ease the fatigue building in my muscles.

Lexi dragged her fingers across my chest, smiling as her hand rested on my heart. She leaned in, nuzzling my sweaty neck and kissing my beard-covered jaw. She purred and desire clouded her gaze when she pulled back.

The song changed from typical line dance to something more primal. The lights dimmed to bare glimpses of bodies among the strobe lights.

Her hand cupped my cheek, before dropping to my chest and around my back as she circled me.

That simple contact racked my body with shivers and desire spiked. I turned to watch her.

Lexi's smile bloomed, rivaling the beauty of the stars at night. Her hair teased me, and I complied, tangling my fingers in the brown locks.

She complied with my silent demand, tilting her head back and willingly surrendered in a kiss.

Underneath the salty taste, she reminded me of our home, surrounded by woods, and the rain falling. Fresh and clean but rich and earthy.

She moaned, as she leaned into me.

We parted, and our chests heaved under the rough hold of desires and more.

The lights were still low, but the beat of the music fueled the need to have more from her.

I braced my arm over her head along one of the support beams near the dance floor.

Her hair caught against the wood, and her lips were still swollen.

I licked my lips, tasting the saltiness of the chips and the earthiness of her.

My scalp tingled, as she wrapped her fingers in my hair, pulling me into another searing kiss. I let my fingers trail along the soft sweater's edge and dip under the hem.

The curve of her hip and the warm, silky-smooth skin that greeted me had me moaning. I couldn't tell where she ended and I began; the sense of touching her fought with the taste of her. And the harder I tried to pay attention to one, the other one dimmed with a sudden feeling of loss.

Piercing cold slid along my neck and down my back. I jerked away from Lexi and turned toward the offending culprit with the ice cubes.

Jackson caught my gaze and smirked. "Go home," he mouthed.

Chapter 24

We lay in bed; Lexi curled alongside me. Her hair spread over my shoulder and across the pillows, mixing with mine.

I kissed her on the forehead and the tip of her nose before laying back against the bed.

She propped herself up on her elbow and nibbled along my neck. Her fingers traced mindless patterns and twirled the dark hair spattered across my chest. She moved to straddle me, but I rolled us to the side.

She gave me a tight-lipped smile. With a sigh, she snuggled in next to me, her arms folded along our chest, her hands clasped under her cheek.

"What's wrong?"

"Nothing," she replied.

I asked again.

This time she shook her head and shifted in my arms.

I pulled the cover over her shoulder, knowing she loved being cocooned in the soft fabric. I traced my hand along her silky-smooth hair and leaned in to kiss her.

She rolled over, facing the door, and scooched back against me. Once or twice she sat up, adjusting the twisted fabric of her shirt.

The warmth from her ass pressed against my groin, stirring the fire in my blood, and I couldn't help pushing back. I kissed her neck, and she pulled away from me.

"What's wrong, Lex.," I whispered in her ear, and inhaled the soft scent of strawberries from her hair.

"Nothing." She shrugged me off.

"Talk to me." I kissed her on one cheek then the other.

She rolled onto her back. Her eyes reflected my own disheveled appearance. "It's stupid. Don't worry about it." She moved to turn back over.

I laid my arm across her chest, sliding my hand under her back and anchoring her in place.

She shook her head and rolled her eyes. She opened her mouth but closed it just as quick. She stared at the blue nightlight in the bathroom instead of me. "Just drop it, Ren."

Shadow poked his nose over the edge of the bed. He stared between us; his tail swishing against the hardwood floor.

"Come on." Lexi tossed the covers aside, letting the chill of the house into the nest of warmth from our bodies and blanket. She scratched the dog on the head and led him out the door.

The front door slammed shut, and the house became silent.

My eyes closed, and I jerked awake. I pulled the blanket over my waist and thought I heard Lexi moving around in the guest room. I laid there, intending to stay awake. But time stretched, and I dozed.

Chapter 25

The bed was empty and cold when I rolled over to turn off the blaring alarm.

I laid back against the sheets. My arm stretched across to the other side.

The house was too quiet. Usually when Lexi was up first, I could hear the coffee pot burble, and her talking to Shadow.

Squinting, I looked at my phone. Five thirty. Maybe Lexi was outside tending to the critter feeders.

I threw the blankets off and headed to the dresser, remembering mid-stride I still didn't have clothes. Grudgingly I threw on last night's apparel and headed to the kitchen.

The coffee pot was full, and the orange light glowed. I poured a cup of coffee and read Lexi's handwritten note—she'd gone to the Laughing P—as I grabbed the milk from the refrigerator. I smiled at the little heart with a line through it she had signed at the bottom.

I drank the coffee and shoved my feet in my boots. Grabbing my hat and keys, I walked out the door.

The trucks lined up against the fence on this wintery day was a stark reminder that nothing stopped when Maw-Payne died. There was still work to be done and a list of things to attend.

My boots resounded against the steps, and ranch hands funneled from the kitchen.

Most nodded in greeting before dispersing across the ranch. Jason and Jeremy chuckled and whispered when they brushed past.

"I'm starting to think you two can't help yourselves." I caught the screen door against my foot and waited for Buddy to amble onto the porch and head toward his food bowl.

Jason slapped his brother on the back, and the duo headed to the barn without another word.

Rick washed dishes. Julie sat in her highchair, babbling *da-da* over and over, as he watched over her. "Plenty of breakfast left over."

"Thanks." I tossed a few biscuits and scrambled eggs on a plate and sat down near the grits. "Breakfast looks good."

"It is. Ronald and Miss Thomas are supposed to be here around eight to go over Maw-Payne's will. I didn't know if Monica had told you." He turned with the dishtowel and scooped the broken biscuits and scrambled eggs, from Julie's highchair top, into the trash can.

"Why Miss Thomas?" I shoved a bite of food in my mouth.

"She's the executor."

A few guys came inside, getting a cup of coffee. Each time, there was a heavier layer of snow flurries clinging to their jackets and their hair.

Rick cleared the table, setting the near empty pot of coffee in front of me.

I sighed and wrapped my hands around the warm cup. Steam rose from the dark surface, and I poured a splash of milk on top of it. The dainty creamer cow *tinked* against the tabletop when I sat it down.

Jason came in, grabbing a radio from the charging station. "I'm heading out with Jeremy to move the chickens to another pen and then rechecking the heat lamps in the barn. Red's got some of the others moving the dairy cows into the field behind the house with the horses."

"Okay." I didn't know why he was telling me any of this. I thought Lexi was handling ranch business again.

"Rick," Jason turned toward my brother-in-law, "Lexi said she wouldn't be back in time to cook lunch, but she had already talked to Lola and Miss Thomas." He tossed his hand up and shrugged, unsure of the specifics of the message.

Jeremy darted in the door and snatched a piece of bacon from the plate on the counter.

Julie giggled, as Rick set her on the floor, and she toddled across the floor toward Jason.

"Hey princess." Jason turned her around and pointed at me. "Why don't you go steal some of your uncle's kisses?"

I picked Julie up and flew her over my head before settling her on my lap. Smiling at her, I resisted the urge of blurting out the apparent obvious statement that Lexi had cooked breakfast.

Maw-Payne had been teaching Monica for years, and to be fair, I wasn't sure Lexi could cook outside camp-fare.

"Where is Lexi?" I played keep-away with Julie, as she reached for my coffee.

Jason and Jeremy exchanged looks. "Haven't seen her since a quarter to six. She's got oh-three if you want to page her." Jason nodded toward the radio charging station.

"I think the better question is, why she was here at four instead of in bed." Jeremy gyrated his hips.

Jason took the thermos Rick held out and nodded his thanks.

"Someone's in the doghouse," the brothers sang off-key and chuckled, going out the door.

I set Julie on the chair next to me and bolted toward the door.

A heavy dusting of snow covered everything. The white flakes fell, and past the fence line, the world looked blah and the high country disappeared.

"Jeremy," I hollered for him.

"You don't have to shout." The spiky-haired man sat on the edge of a rocking chair, petting Buddy and Shadow.

"It's been a long few days, can we skip the proverbial bush?"

He braced his arm against his thigh, scratching the dog's ears—Buddy's foot thumped against the wooden planks, and he languidly slumped to the floor.

Shadow turned and gazed out across the yard. His ears twitched, listening. Lightning quick, he darted from the porch and disappeared in the grey morning light.

Jeremy stood and braced against the porch railing, watching his brother roll the moveable chicken pen toward the porch. "You didn't hear this from me." His brow wrinkled, as he thought about what he was going to say. "The morning I went over there, she was asleep on the couch. Now I don't know about you, but if I was a betting man, I'd wager she hadn't slept in that new bed the last few nights." He dashed down the couple of steps and paused. Looking at me, he spoke, "Don't forget your clothes when you go home."

I watched the snow flurries, taking their sweet time falling before the chill seeped through my long-sleeve shirt. I stomped my feet against the mat out of habit and yanked the screen door open.

Rick had the phone shoved against his shoulder and juggled little Ethan, who was screaming for something. "I'll let him know." He hung the phone up and sighed. He closed his eyes, oblivious to me, and ground his jaw. "Ethan, hush already. I will get you breakfast," he snapped.

In a moment of remorse, he leaned his forehead against Ethan's and tried to gather himself. "Sorry, little man. Not your fault daddy doesn't know your schedule."

He adjusted Ethan against his hip and turned toward me. He startled as he saw me, and his shoulders sagged. "Miss Thomas called. She's already on the way here."

I ran my fingers through my hair and ran my hands down my face.

Could Maw-Payne make a more complicated will? Knowing the old woman all my life, probably.

I picked my hat off the seat and slid from the truck. The duffle bag caught against the edge of the toolbox when I reached over the truck bed's rail and picked up the bag. With a solid yank, the bag gave way, and the strap smacked against my arm.

At least Monica was set that made me happy. She had the Laughing P house and the garden through the dairy cow acres. A decent little spread to do the guest ranch from.

The kitchen light illuminated the snow-covered window, and Lexi's shadow danced on the curtain.

I eased the screen door open, unsure if *nothing* still bothered her.

Shadow stood on his back feet. His front paws rested in Lexi's hands.

Lexi's hair flowed around her, as she moved, and her voice sounded heavenly as she sang.

The timer dinged, and she eased Shadow down and turned toward the stove. She removed a pan from the oven and reached over the burners, turning off the knobs.

Shadow waited to see if he would get a piece of food before he turned his solid black eyes toward me. His nails clacked against the floor when he dashed toward me.

"How's Monica?" She leaned over the stove top and tasted a sauce.

"She didn't lock herself up in Maw-Payne's room … again." I set the bag against the side table. "Dinner smells good."

"Thanks." Her voice was an even tone and distant. She spooned something over rice and set the plate on the bar.

"Need any help?" I took a step toward the silverware drawer.

"No, thank you. Your fork is next to your plate." She tossed the big spoon into the sink, and balanced her plate and fork in one hand.

She raised an eyebrow and stared at me.

I looked around, curious as to what she was waiting on.

"Can you move, please?" She gave me a soft smile and nodded when I sidestepped. "Thanks."

Her plate *tinked* against the counter, and Shadow swiveled his head, his gaze searching for a dropped crumb. He crossed his paws and laid his head on top of them.

"Smells good." I sat on the bar stool beside her.

"You already said that," she chuckled in reply. Her fork pushed against the rice and gravy, mixing the two together.

Rice and gravy weren't that atypical, but the chicken breast was rolled and topped with melted cheese. I cut the chicken in half, and white cheese and something green oozed from the dissection.

I stabbed the small piece with a fork and looked at the stuffing.

"It's feta and spinach. If you don't like it, there's leftovers from the last few nights in the fridge." She turned her plate to begin eating her chicken.

I smirked at her idiosyncrasies.

She was the only person I knew who ate one complete item from her plate before rotating to the next.

She didn't try to fill the silence. We ate dinner, and like so many nights before, we cleaned the kitchen, this time loading the new dishwasher.

I caught myself staring at her. New jeans hugged the curve of her hips. Her long hair swished across her shoulders as she moved, and the overhead lights made her hair glisten like topaz gems spun into strands.

She let Shadow out, and filled his food bowl while chastising him for being a rambunctious pup and chasing the night critters.

I poured a cup of coffee. A nagging feeling grew, furrowing my brow.

"I know that look. What are you concentrating on so hard?" She passed me the milk before refilling her glass.

I shook my head, my hair falling across my face. "I feel like I've forgotten something."

She shrugged and smirked. "Grandma always said if you couldn't remember something, it must have been a lie."

I rolled up my sleeves and watched her eyes flash with a different type of hunger.

"What?"

"Nothing." As quick as the desire bloomed, she shut down.

I cornered her against the counter, trapping her between my arms. I was tired of watching her deny the things she wanted, afraid of asking for anything and everything she deserved.

"Is it nothing now?"

She refused to look at me.

I tucked her hair behind her ear, watching the pulse hammer against her neck.

The top of her shirt fluttered with each quick breath, and her lips parted, trying to ease the heat growing in her.

Her gaze focused on my exposed arms. Her finger traced the thick lines along the edge of my tattoos, and her breathing hitched. She licked her lips and swallowed.

Her sea-green eyes met my gaze, and I captured her lips, determined to brand her like I should have nights ago.

Chapter 26

My arm laid across her smooth back, tracing absentminded patterns along her side and the swell of her ass.

Lexi peered through a curtain of hair and smiled languidly. Her eyes drifted closed a second, before she laid her head on top of her crossed arms.

I kissed her elbow then her shoulder.

She moaned low and deep, turning her face toward me, and that languid smile vanished, replaced with a mischievous grin demanding a second helping.

Her arm snaked around my neck and pulled me toward her.

The front door banged open, and all-too-familiar voices filled the house.

"What the fuck!" I rolled onto my back, intent on chasing the hoodlums from the house.

"It's your bachelor party. Go have fun." She slid from the bed, snatching the blanket from round me and wrapping it around her. She blew me a kiss and disappeared into the bathroom.

I fumbled for my boxers and barely got them pulled over my ass, before the Hardy boys popped their heads into the bedroom.

"Don't you know how to knock," I snapped at them.

"Looking for these?" Jason held my jeans by a belt loop before tossing them to me. "Get dressed."

The fire crackled in the field behind the Mistwood homestead.

I kept glancing in the direction of the house, but the fifteen-minute drive had put it out of sight behind a knoll. The same one Lexi and I had chased each other across on our way to the gazebo.

"Come on, lighten up." Lionel raised his beer in a toast. He was the exact opposite of Richie. Star track athlete in high school, he hadn't let the sedate pace of the town curb his physique.

I nearly choked on my Coke as a coughing fit erupted. The wind shifted, unexpectedly blowing bonfire smoke down my windpipe.

"Don't you guys know not to interrupt a man when he's—"

Jason interrupted Jackson, singing "Bow-chicka wow-wow." He gyrated his hips and laughed when the others joined in.

"How were we supposed to know?" Charles slapped me on the back, jostling me forward and knocking Coke all over my hand.

I shook my hand off and wiped the lingering drops on my jeans. Even bundled in a jacket and standing near the fire, winter's bite seeped to my core.

Across the gentle rolls of fields surrounded by trees, the snow glistened in the moonlight that escaped through dispersing clouds. Nothing aside from the playful antics of the group and the fire's steady crackling sounded in the night.

We didn't need music, but it would have helped to drown out the stupid one-liner jokes and the slow ticking minutes until I could leave.

I settled against the tailgate happy that the guys hadn't dragged me two towns over to go to the strip club.

Sawyer walked over and pulled himself up on Red's tailgate. "Isn't the whole bachelor party supposed to be you having fun and being embarrassed?" He looked around and smirked. "If I didn't know any better, I'd say this was Rick's party."

I scanned the group at the mention of my brother-in-law's name and wasn't disappointed.

He could barely stand up straight, being drunker than a skunk. His hand wavered, as he squinted. He tried to toss the horseshoe. He threw wide, and the cast iron shoe landed in the fire, sending sparks up in its wake.

The onlookers laughed, encouraging Rick to try again.

"Better him than me," I muttered.

Rick needed the break. Between handling chores he never had to do, and stepping up for Monica and the twins, he was about one request short of blowing his top.

"You didn't hear it from me, but your brother-in-law is the new town lawyer. Ronald's taking over for Pritchard." Sawyer took a sip.

I scratched my beard. It didn't surprise me he got the job. But people were fickle in town, and he'd be lucky, if he they accepted him immediately.

"Thought I saw Damien at the bar last night." Sawyer fidgeted with the pants leg around his prosthetic.

I leaned my head back against the bed railing. The last lie I told Maw-Payne filtered through, drowning out the party. I pulled my phone out of my pocket and tapped the plastic against my knee.

Damien's phone went straight to voicemail every time I'd called since Maw-Payne died.

I flipped the screen up and pressed contacts. His name looked no different than any others on the list, but I dreaded calling him. What would I say if he picked up?

The icon changed to a loading circle before flashing "end". We were too far from the cell towers to get any reception.

"Turns out it was one of Steve's new recruits." Sawyer drummed his fingers against his thigh.

I finished my drink and crinkled the can, tossing it toward the cab.

"Why don't you go on home?" Sawyer patted my knee and hopped off the tailgate.

Chapter 27

I pored over a topographical map of the county. From the National Park through to the North county line, I tried to find reason for Maw-Payne's final decree.

She had given Monica the lands from the dairy cows through the house and adjacent buildings for the guest ranch. That made sense since the first reading, and I had no reason to argue. Eldest born, Monica could have ended up with the entire ranch.

We had waited thirty days to hear the rest of the will, and it boggled my mind. The land to the west of the winding river, about twenty percent of the Laughing P, went to Lexi for going above and beyond, when she paid off a debt larger than I had even known about.

The remaining land of the Laughing P was a strip of timber-covered land, flanking the cattle drive grazing land that bordered the parcel given to Lexi. Any profits made from that rocky land was to be split between Damien and me.

My finger rested over the grazing lands … my land. In a good rainy season, the fields could stay knee deep in grass, growing quicker than the cows could graze it flush.

I glanced out the window at the green grass.

Spring seemed far away, with the constant snow and freezing temperatures, but had rounded third and headed toward home plate, chasing the harsh winter away, and the rye had already started to reach through the soil.

The calendar peered out from beneath the map, and I covered the bright blue circle around it. The reminder of Doc's annual physical didn't ease the knot in my gut. Neither did the giant red heart Monica had scribbled around today.

Valentine's Day. I looked at the scribbled list I had scratched through in the last two weeks. Nothing seemed like a good fit for our first Valentine's Day.

My phone rang. "Jeremy" flashed on the screen, and I hit the end button. If it was important, they'd call Lexi. My phone chimed again with a voice message. I clicked the side button, effectively silencing the blasted thing.

I rubbed my eyes and sat at the desk. There had to have been a reason Maw-Payne had made the stipulations to break up the Laughing P. Did she think Damien wouldn't be around? Was this something she decided on before Granddaddy died?

"A little guidance wouldn't hurt," I muttered. My head *thumped* against the desk. I was tired. Tired of worrying about Damien. Tired of not knowing anything.

My eyes drifted shut, and the only solid idea was I should tell Lexi about it before someone else did.

I couldn't have dozed long. The sun shone still bright through the window when the office door banged open.

Rick leaned over, huffing and coughing. "Don't you know how to answer a damn phone?"

I looked at my cell, seeing the screen flash "missed calls." The house phone on the edge of the desk hung off the hook.

"What happened?" I stretched, wondering what the emergency was while my mind awoke.

"Get your ass to the hospital."

The town doctor and the veterinarian shared the same building, each working opposite ends. Usually just a few vehicles dotted the spacious parking lot, but two passes through, and I couldn't find a parking space.

Near the emergency entrance, I pulled my truck up on the curb, making sure I didn't block access to the emergency bay. Snatching my hat from the seat, I bolted through the doors.

A mass of people filled the simple hallway, spilling from the waiting room and into vacant rooms.

Heads turned, and some breathed a sigh of relief.

I pushed through the throng of bodies, going where a few nodded.

Jason and Jeremy leaned against the doorjamb to keep people out of the tiny room.

Lexi clutched Red's hand against the white sheets. She refused to turn her gaze from him.

His withered hand stroked her cheek, catching a tear. "Lexi. It'll be okay."

"No. You can fight this." Her voice trembled, and my throat knotted.

"Child." He coughed. "When you get as old as me, you don't want to linger."

She straightened her shoulders before leaning closer. "You knew."

Disbelief spread through the crowd.

"Maw-Payne promised she wouldn't tell. Who knew she'd go first?" He tried to chuckle, but the wet cough made him gasp for air.

He eased back against the pillow and took the suctioning tube from the nurse. His old grey eyes, surrounded by wrinkles and red skin, closed for a moment, and a collective gasp flowed as the onlookers thought it was his last.

The nurse tried to put the oxygen mask over his face, but he batted it away.

I watched the IV-infused hand grasp Lexi's. As much as I wanted to be beside her, I couldn't bring myself to intrude.

In hushed tones, their words turned from English to a form of Cherokee dialect I couldn't follow.

He insisted on something, and tears poured from her face. She nodded fiercely. "I will."

He coughed blood into the gauze he held. The nurse wiped at his mouth, and he squeezed her hand, shaking his head no.

She nodded and left the bedside, pushing past she hollered for Doctor McGee.

His name passed on muttering lips. We turned, looking for the man with sway over life and death.

The machines began to code, beeping erratically.

My gaze anchored on Lexi, unsure of how to help her.

An anguishing cry tore from Lexi, silencing the rustling of bodies.

Doc McGee squeezed by, intent on doing something I couldn't see.

Lexi's hand shot out lightning fast, anchoring to McGee's wrist. She shook her head. Her hair swished fiercely in her opposition. "It's not what he wanted."

Doc hesitated. "I'm just silencing the machines." He patted her hand until she let go. He flipped the machine off. Seconds past, and he dictated the time.

Tears flowed freely, and my chest ached.

Jason turned and bumped me. "How long have you been here?" He was unabashed to be crying like everyone else.

"Not long enough."

"Does he have any kin?" McGee wiped his eye and picked up the pen to write again.

Lexi paused at the door, unaware of us. "No. Unless you have something I don't know about, I want him buried with Grandma and Grandpa. I think that's what he would want." She bit down on her lip, trying to silence the whimpering that threaten to erupt in place of her tears, the same look I'd seen when her grandparents died.

Glossy eyed, she blinked and looked at everyone. Lost for words, she shook her head, pushed past me, and fled out the emergency exit.

A resounding *We remember* followed in our wake as I chased after her.

Chapter 28

Just before the cover of the oaks gave way, I turned onto a secondary road leading to the ranch hand bungalows.

Red's was the last one on the right. I passed three others in the process.

The brakes squeaked, as my truck came to a stop. I turned the key and sat.

Red's truck sat next to the stack of firewood. It looked freshly washed, lacking the pollen coating everything else wore.

I yanked the band from my hair and reached for the brush under the seat. I needed a moment to figure out what I was going to say.

First Maw-Payne and now Red? He had been a constant for nearly two decades.

I rubbed my hands against my face and exhaled, gathering myself to face whatever I found. My ponytail flopped against my neck. I slid out of the truck and left my hat on the seat.

Rock music blared throughout the small house, and I paused at the open door.

She had bolted from the hospital, and only a trail of dust had let me know where she went. Did she even want me here?

In all the years Red had lived here, I'd never been inside.

Overhead lights illuminated the open space, revealing more about the man I had called friend.

Barely furnished, a leather couch sat in front of the television. The right seat showed cracks in the leather, and the armrest was worn to a lighter color. A floor lamp stood in the corner of the room, and one of its frosted-glass shades was missing a bulb while the other two arms swiveled to highlight the kitchen table.

I touched the table top, seeing plans for a bunkhouse with Red's tight handwriting scribbled around the edges of the page. I fingered the bright flowers sitting in the vase, and wondered if Lexi had brought them over.

The walls were filled with compositions of wide open fields dotted with livestock and bucking broncos, and squeezed around the fireplace, pictures of us throughout the years hung against the blue walls. Lexi's signature graced the bottom of each picture, and brass plates rested on the three-inch-wide, white mats.

I followed the *oldies* down the hallway. The first bedroom was an office with a pull-out sofa nestled under the window. A thin metal desk rested against the short wall, a neat stack of printer paper and a printer its only inhabits.

A light-colored foot from a kitchen chair jutted across the open doorway.

Lexi sat hunched over, looking inside a small, thin box. Trash bags littered the room in various stages of fulfillment. The closet had been emptied, and Red's signature winter jacket laid across the bed.

"This stuff could wait, Lex." I kneeled beside her.

Instead of tears, she smiled and showed me the collection of doodads.

I picked up a broken button and dropped the plastic back among the others. A bent nail and a piece of cloth, nothing that would make sense to me, made her smile.

She closed the box and tossed it in the trash can.

"Wait, what?" I searched her face, expecting rage or anger.

"He kept things that I don't even remember the importance of. They were things that I gave him over the years." Her eyes squinted, as she tried to pry memories long faded from her thoughts. "It's enough knowing he kept them."

She stood from the chair and walked to the side table. Her fingers pushed against the glasses sitting on top of a book, toppling them from their perch.

Without words, tears fell down her cheeks, and in those moments, she pulled a dresser drawer from its hold and folded stacks of shirts into a trash bag, using her hurt as fuel. As quick as the crystal-clear drops had covered her face, they stopped, and she smiled at some memory.

"Every Sunday, he'd pick-up fresh flowers." She pulled something from the top drawer. She set the faded box on the bed, and the top popped off, displaying military ribbons and a coin.

She pulled her phone from her back pocket. Her gaze narrowed, as she scrolled through her contacts. Her thumb hovered over the screen. With a tiny shake of her head, she typed out a text message instead.

"Did you know Red was one of the liberators of some of the bigger concentration camps in World War Two?" Not waiting for a reply, she spoke of the honor and privilege of knowing a man who willingly saw the worst in humanity fight to show others the light.

The tears began to flow again, and she buzzed around the room, taking her turmoil out on the closest area of the room, instead of systematically like she handled so many things.

I sat in the vacant chair and watched her war with her emotions. The more she cleared of Red's room, the more I wondered, if cleaning out Maw-Payne and Granddaddy's room would be just as therapeutic.

Chapter 29

Red's funeral was tomorrow morning in the town cemetery. But Lexi and I stood on a knoll overlooking the rolling fields of Mistwood, stretching for miles beneath cloudy skies, and listening to the backhoe grind and dig into the hard, red clay.

I hadn't realized that the tombstones in the town cemetery were all for show.

I stared down at a tombstone marked with Chatan and Pam's names. *Eternal Love* stretched beneath their names and the flowing ribbon framed the dates of their lives. It didn't seem that long ago that they both died, but a decade had passed for Chatan and nearly that for Pam.

On the right side of the large granite marker, a solitary stone stood, looking worn and discolored compared to the larger one. *Loving son. Devoted father. Gone too soon.*

Lexi leaned on the edge of the stone and crossed her ankles. "Hey Dad. I miss you." She fingered the top of the etched words. "I don't know, if you remember Ren or not. I think you'd like him."

Wind whipped through her hair, spreading the dark brown locks out. She pushed off the stone. A smile blossomed on her face, even with her eyes glossed over, with unshed tears. She kissed her fingers and touched the top of the stone.

She pressed herself along my back. Her arms slipped under mine, and her fingers grasped my collarbone. She kissed my shoulder and sighed. "I love you, Ren."

Doc McGee hollered for her.

Our hands trailed down each other's arms and our fingers lingered across our palms. With a tight-lipped smile, she walked toward McGee.

Picking up a handful of clay, she tossed it on top of the casket and a large chunk bounced, before dropping off into the dark hole below.

I slipped my hand around her hand and, without words, provided whatever support she might need, just as she had done for me when Maw-Payne had passed.

Looking out past the backhoe, this was exactly the type of place Red would want to be buried.

"I wanted to tell you, Lexi, I argued with Red to do the treatment."

Lexi held her hand up, stopping McGee from saying any more. "He made his choice. Lung cancer isn't pretty, and he went on his terms. How many people get to say that?" She smiled, but a tear rolled off the tip of her nose. "You can finish up here?" She asked the man wielding the backhoe controls.

He nodded and offered a sad smile.

She mouthed, "Thank you," and we walked toward the ATV.

I climbed on behind her, letting her lead us to wherever she needed to go.

Instead of across the open fields, she turned toward home.

Shadow barked and loped after us when we rumbled over the cattle guard. He paused where Lexi parked and tilted his head in expectation of being petted.

Silence descended on the yard as she turned the key. She sat there, leaning her arms across the handle bars.

I rubbed her shoulders, squeezing occasionally.

She sighed, satisfied with whatever decision she had chosen. Sitting up, she threw a leg over the seat and hopped off. She turned toward me and glanced at the house. With a soft smile that didn't quiet reach her eyes, she asked, "You coming?"

Chapter 30

I leaned over Sawyer's work table. The blueprints were easier to read on the backlighted table, but Red's handwriting became a glowing mess of ink.

"The plans are solid. Any idea where he was talking about building this?" Sawyer sat back on the stool and set his glasses on top of his head.

I shook my head. "No. I didn't want to ask Lexi until after I talked to you. I was thinking if this worked, Monica could use the current bunkhouse for her guest ranch, and that would relocate the majority of the actual ranch responsibilities to the Mistwood."

Sawyer rubbed his lips and thought. "It's been awhile since I was there, but isn't that front field between Laughing P and Mistwood clear cut? Could put it there, and then it's a central location." He shrugged. "Ultimately, you're going to have to pull the money from somewhere. You're talking about a massive septic tank and judging from this design two rooms per bathroom—" He counted the rooms. "—nine, no ten bathrooms, and a kitchen. Not cheap."

I knew that. The renovation to the house had cost more than I had expected, but if I had the timber cut, the expected pay would cover the structure. One tiny problem, I'd owe Damien a lot of money.

Sawyer unscrewed the water bottle lid and took a sip of water. "Sorry to hear about Red. How is Lexi handling it?"

"Honestly, I don't have a clue."

His rich laugh filled the shop. "Seems like you been getting plenty of action. Didn't your daddy ever teach you concealer?" Sawyer pulled at the collar of my shirt and whistled. "Some of the nicest hickies I ever saw."

I scrambled back a step and tugged on my shirt. My ears felt hot as I blushed.

Sawyer laughed some more. "Sex is normal you know. The dead don't care."

I stared at the man. A snicker escaped turning into a deep belly laugh. With each deep chuckle, a weight I hadn't realized I had been carrying evaporated.

"Feel better?" Sawyer rolled up the blueprints and fed them into the cardboard tube. The black plastic cap scraped against the top before popping snuggly into place.

My hands rested on my hips, and the 9mm holster dug into my side. Standing, trying to stop the burning in my lungs, I realized what *nothing* had been about.

Nothing had been more than just me wanting to cuddle. It was me being stupid on so many levels. We were dealing with a loss of Maw-Payne and ten million other things the first night we'd spent together married.

"Better than I could have imagined."

Sex was a way for two people to talk without ever saying a word, and I had silenced her without meaning to.

Red and Maw-Payne both would want us to live, laugh, and love.

"Good, now how about we finish that crib for the Andersons?"

I combed my fingers through my hair and pulled the locks into a messy bun. With a smirk on my face and a spring in my step, I picked up the sandpaper and began to run the spindles through the fine grit paper.

Someday I'd be building one of these for Lexi and me.

Chapter 31

I leaned over the edge of the truck bed and pulled a water bottle from the cooler. Despite March's weather mood-swings, today was hot. I stuck my head over, before pouring half the bottle over my head. A lone trickle chased the beads of sweat, and I gasped, as the chill streaked across my chest, clinging to the damp shirt.

The constant swing of hammers and saws made my head hurt, but admiring the new bunkhouse slowly come together made it worth it.

Ranch hands hustled back and forth across the construction strewn yard. An almost musical quality followed the string of cussing as something slipped and another jammed.

The generators kicked off, bringing a resounding silence to the field.

Almost as one, the men turned and stared. Their gaze riveted to a spot behind me.

Seconds ticked by, before I heard the slam of Lexi's truck door.

She slid her hands up over my shoulder blades and around to my chest, before she snaked her hands around my waist, and standing on tiptoes, tried to kiss my neck.

"Afternoon, Lex." I encircled her with my free arm, bringing her around to the front. I captured her lips in a quick kiss.

Too late, the chorus of hollers and whistles erupted as the men rushed toward the packed coolers loaded with lunch.

"They just like seeing you squirm. If you'd stop turning so red, they'd stop." She whispered in my ear. She detangled herself from my embrace and took a step back.

"Who said I want to stop?" I caught her hand and twirled her back in my arms, stealing a kiss that filled her gaze with desire.

"Don't start something you aren't prepared to finish." Her nails glided down my back, and I shuddered. She winked and moved away to help control the hungry men.

The line moved sluggishly. One moment the guys were fighting over sandwiches, and the next Lexi had the men using their manners, making sure each worker got a sandwich or two, chips, and ice cold sweet tea.

She raised her head, her braid falling around her shoulder, and that shy smile was just for me.

I stepped up and surveyed the various coolers. They were empty.

The truck bobbed, as Lexi jumped from the tailgate. "I didn't forget about you." She grabbed my hand, leading me to the cab. "I just thought you'd like a picnic?"

Nestled on the seat was Maw-Payne's picnic basket with the worn, discolored wicker sides and the blue gingham fabric lining the inside.

"I know you guys haven't cleared out her room yet, but I didn't think you would mind if we used the basket that we never took back." She leaned against the truck door, and her shoulders sagged with each passing second.

Wow. I hadn't expected her to do this.

I raised the lid on the basket and smiled at the container filled with supreme pizza and a gallon of sweet tea.

She squeezed past me, and I realized I hadn't said anything.

"It's perfect, Lex. Just what I wanted." My fingers wrapped around her arm, bringing her back to me.

For a second, the steely look of defiance flashed in her gaze. In the next breath, the tension left her shoulders, and she forced a smile.

"I'm sorry. I didn't think."

She patted my hand before wrapping her hands around it. "I don't want you to think. I don't want you to worry about anything other than loving me."

She laid my hand on her waist. Her fingers climbed over my sleeve and along my bicep. She wrapped her arms around my neck, pulling me closer.

"Now shut up, and kiss me." She smiled before capturing my lip between her teeth, nibbling along the tender flesh and tugging on things that were soul deep.

I hefted the basket and followed her lead, as she led us under the sprawling oak, with its budding leaves and its pollen producing tinsel.

Instead of waiting for me to pull the blanket out of the basket, she sat against the trunk and crossed her ankles.

I eased down beside her, taking residence between the massive knotted roots protruding from the ground. I offered her a slice of pizza, and at her dismissive nod, I shrugged before digging in.

Despite the road being within shouting distance, the view was spectacular. The Laughing P's front fields stretched behind the bunkhouse's frame, culminating in the Laughing P homestead flanked by grazing fields and livestock. The same view the bunkhouse would have from the porch when it was finished.

"We need to pick a ranch manager. Not just for us, but one for Monica's guest ranch too."

It was a hard balance between owner and manager, and neither of us could be everywhere. I picked at a green pepper, hesitant to admit I had been thinking the same long before Red died.

We could keep going like we were, being multiple parts of the cog, but that didn't make the ranch work any better.

"Who?"

"Carlos for Monica." She leaned her head against my shoulder and closed her eyes. "I couldn't decide between the Hardys. They've been here since they were sixteen." Her words were swallowed by a yawn.

"Zeb and Zeke were going to split it, so why not them?"

Thinking of the brothers we lost last summer made me chuckle at their grizzled hair appearance, reminding me of a hermit living off the grid, and the constant competition between the pair.

"Hmmm-hmmm." Lexi's head dropped against my arm and she shifted against my shoulder before sleep took her again.

I wrapped my arm around her, and settled in against the tree.

Chapter 32

Pain radiated from my back as I pulled another line of wire through the studs. I flexed my gloved hands, easing the cramps from them. Ranch work was hard, but building a house took a whole other set of skills and muscles, and my body protested at the unusual workload.

"You sure you don't want us to stay?" Jason picked up a yellow hard hat and tossed it in the air, catching it like a football.

"Nah, I'm just going to finish this little bit of line for the inspection tomorrow." I yanked the wire through the blue electrical box secured to the post. "Besides, y'all worked in the afternoon, while I got to sit in the nice shade." I smirked.

I'd enjoyed the two-hour break. Lexi had slept, and I couldn't bring myself to wake her, instead guiding her to lay her head in my lap while stroking her hair.

"True," Jason laughed. "Save some of the work for us. I'll see you at breakfast."

I nodded to the Hardys.

I watched his lights disappear down the improvised driveway, before I killed the last generator. Darkness descended upon the worksite, drawing to a standstill around two LED lanterns that glowed.

I sat on a stack of drywall. The bottle cap popped off the water bottle and rolled across the floor, leaving a wavering line in the dust.

Staring at the frames and seeing the electrical running through the walls helped me visualize how it would look, when we finished in a couple of weeks. More spacious than the current bunkhouse. Each of the guys could have privacy, and the common area and kitchen would be spectacular.

I wasn't sure how or when I could pay Damien back, but that was a problem for another day.

My gloves landed by my shoes, and I dug in my back pocket, pulling out my phone. The screen awoke, and I scrolled to Damien's name. Had he listened to any of the messages I had left since Maw-Payne passed? Or had he just deleted them, never knowing of the tragedy that struck our family?

The loading circle turned green, and I waited for the familiar monotone voice mail. "Hey, Damien. It's Darien. I don't know if you've listened to the last dozen or hundred messages we've left since Christmas. At least text me when you can. We—I just need to know that you're okay." I clicked end just as the beep sounded, noting the end of the message.

I scrolled to Lexi's number and texted her I'd be home in an hour or so. I picked my gloves. The wire wouldn't pull itself.

I fed the strand through the studs, pulling it around to the next receptacle box. The wooden reel shifted across the floor as the last of the wire unwound. The end flopped against the ground, before it caught against a two-by-four.

I fumbled through the gloves for the wire strippers. With steady pressure, I stripped the red and black lines and twisted the similar ends of another cable, before securing the copper ends against the receptacle screws.

A board creaked, and I paused with the screwdriver in hand.

"Lex? That you?" Was she surprising me again?

I couldn't see anything outside the glow of the battery powered lantern, but someone moved near the common area.

"There's a light near the door." I hollered.

Silence greeted me.

The hairs on the back of my neck prickled. "Lex? Jason? Jeremy?" My eyes searched the dark, trying to find the silhouette.

A scrape of feet against the concrete floor had me turning in a circle. I reached for my 9mm and realized I had left it in the truck. The screwdriver became my only line of defense

I turned in time to see a scrap piece of a two-by-four come out of the dark and pain blossom into nothingness.

I grunted, as I came to. My eyes fluttered open, and the movement tugged at the blood that had congealed on my right side. I tugged my shoulder forward, coming to an abrupt stop as a nylon tie-down strap anchored me to the four-by-four secured to the floor. My cough tore through the night, and my ribs hurt.

"Where's Dami?" The rough, brittle voice made my head throb.

I squinted at the edge of the light, and the hunched over human shape moved.

"Donna?" I shifted against the post.

The thing I had forgotten about was standing before me.

"You know where he is. I heard you on the phone. Where is he?" She lunged toward me, and the light revealed a haggard woman.

Her once blonde hair became sucked into the void of her dark roots. Dirt and thin scratches marked her face, and the once perfectly done blue eyes were missing the colored contacts, and brown and crazed eyes stared back at me.

She held the end of the screwdriver against my throat. Cautiously she leaned in, sniffing my neck.

"Where is he?" Her free hand pulled up the base of my shirt before she reached into my pockets.

"Phone. Phone. Phone," she mumbled over and over, lost in her world.

She pounded against the side of her head and moved away from me, empty-handed of her prize.

"I saw you. The day after I escaped." She shifted her hold on the screwdriver as she became more in control, and my pulse sped. "Pounding into your wife on the office desk. You should learn to lock doors. That look of utter joy across both of your faces. Maybe I went after the wrong brother. You're obviously the more fulfilling one" She shook her head. "No. No. No." She pounded the side of her head again and wrapped her fingers in the thin strands. She hobbled away from the light.

I pulled against the board and against the strap. The straps were made to hold thousands of pounds, but there had to be a way out. Maybe I could reach my phone.

"I thought Lexi knew where Damien was. It was a disappointment when I learned she didn't. What do you Paynes see in her? She isn't perfection."

"If you hurt Lex," my words faltered, as Donna's voice changed pitch again.

"I'm not perfection now." She turned her hands over in the artificial light. "My beautiful hair." She cried, as her fingers curled into her dingy hair. "My perfect skin!" She covered her face with her hands, and a sob echoed against the night.

As quick as the tears came they stopped. Cackling laughter filled the air, and the sounds of the night fled in its wake.

Her smile had at times been a forced perfection, but the curl of her irregular grin made my stomach drop. She marched out of the light more in control than she had been, and that scared me more than the crazy version.

"I heard about Damien trying to cleanse his soul with fire."

The gas swished against the plastic sides as she shook the red can. Gas sputtered from the black spout, soaking into the wooden frame and the stacked lumber. She worked her way closer and closer toward me. The foul smell burned my lungs, and I began to cough.

"Donna, don't do this." Blood began to ooze through the semi-clotted wound and dripped against my arm.

She drenched my jeans in the gas.

I closed my eyes, hating that I'd never see Lexi again. I'd never see our child. Monica and Rick with their twins flashed through my mind. Jason and Jeremy and all the antics those two managed to get into without trying.

I heard the strike of the match against the box, and I couldn't stop from looking at the beast of fire that consumed without pause.

Donna's ragged clothes had been sloshed with gas. She walked closer toward me, keeping the flame dancing along the small match.

"I changed my mind about killing Lexi. Killing you will result in the same."

I couldn't tell which side of her was in control—the fragmented woman with no hope, or the crazed woman with nothing to lose but vengeance.

"Donna. Don't do this."

Both our heads jerked up.

Donna's broken smile became filled with awe. "Dami," she whispered.

He carefully stepped over some stacked boards and came into the light. He clutched my 9mm and kept his sights on Donna. His hair was buzzed, and his clothes fit better than they had three months ago.

"You okay, Darien?" He didn't risk a glance in my direction.

"I've been better."

Donna took a step forward, and the match dropped from her hand. The flame was caught between dying and fighting to live. The stick bounced against her leg and landed on the floor.

I held my breath, hoping that the flame had suffocated.

A second ticked agonizingly slow, before I sighed against the post.

"Donna, get on your knees." Damien was precise, giving her commands, one step at a time.

Keeping the barrel on her, he eased near me and squatted against the post. His hand fumbled behind me for the ratchet. The metal ground against itself, as he opened the teeth, allowing the strap to slide free. He pulled on the strap and wrapped a hand around my arm, easing me to stand.

"Nasty cut. Here." He pulled a bandana from his pocket and pressed it against my hand.

"Occupational hazard." I stepped out of my prison, and my head spun.

"Can you call Mull?" He risked a glance at me. "You might need to sit down."

"In a minute." I didn't have to visit Doc McGee to know I had a concussion. I reached in my back pocket and punched in Nancy's cell number.

On the second ring, a grumpy Nancy answered the phone. "It better be good, Payne."

"Miss Nancy, can you send a squad car to pick up Donna?" I tried to move to another stud, and nearly fell between the sixteen-inch gap. "And McGee would be nice too." I slid against the board, my shirt catching against the wood, and I sat on the cold concrete.

Chapter 33

Lights filled the night, but I stared into the woods. I hissed, as Doc cleaned up the gash from the two-by-four.

"I'm going to need to stitch that up."

Lexi stayed anchored to my side, holding my hand in a death grip. Armed to the teeth, she had arrived minutes after Damien had secured Donna with a zip tie we had laying around.

She leaned across the tailgate and pulled out the Maglite. "We both know he won't go to the hospital without someone's foot up his ass."

Doc cleared his throat and smirked. "It's a common Payne trait. You'll get used to it."

She cupped my face, searching my gaze. "I wouldn't change a hair on his head." She kissed me softly and moved, giving room for Doc to start.

The needle bit into my flesh around my temple, but the pounding headache drowned it out. The stitching string felt weird gliding through my skin, and I wished the numbing agent would have kicked in a little quicker.

I wanted to sleep.

"Not yet, Darien." Doc tugged on the line, tying a knot. "You know the rules."

I opened my eyes. Bringing Lexi's hand to my lips, I kissed the back of her hand.

She sighed and smiled, finally finding some ease in the moment.

"Swing by the office tomorrow, and I'll have the antibiotic prescriptions waiting at the front. He's going to be on antibiotics for ten days, and it'll be a week before I want him moving around too much. Concussions can ..."

I tuned Doc out and closed my eyes again.

"Thanks Doc." Lexi squeezed my hand. She leaned over, kissing where my beard stopped along my cheek. "I'm going to give you two a minute." She moved away, giving me some privacy.

I shifted against the side of the truck bed where the tailgate's catch line anchored, trying to get comfortable.

Damien cleared his throat. His thumbs hooked in his jeans pockets. "I'm sorry I didn't get here sooner."

"We're glad you're home." I patted him on the shoulder before leaning against the truck bed again. A cough tore through me, making me wince as pain radiated across my skull.

I slid off the tailgate. Stretching my ribs didn't ease the pain, but the nagging feeling of needing to cough dissipated.

"I'm sorry I wasn't here when Maw-Payne died. I went to rehab for thirty days and didn't get the messages until the end of January." He rushed to explain. "I know it won't change anything, but I'm sorry. Sorry for a lot of things."

I pulled him into a hug. "It's never too late to start over. I'm just glad you're okay." Tears prickled my eyes.

We broke apart. Our hands rested against both our necks, reminding me of our high school football days and psyching each other up before a big game.

He turned my head, appraising Doc's handiwork. "She cracked you good with a stick."

I grunted and sat down. "Family trait. I remember you had a nasty one from a baseball bat."

"Where is Red at?"

Taken aback, I stared dumbfounded at him. He knew so much but not everything.

"You're going to want to sit down." I cleared my throat before telling him the news.

His gaze focused against the night sky, where the trees couldn't touch the stars. "I didn't know. I got all your messages about Maw-Payne, but—wow."

Lexi materialized out of nowhere, holding two cups of steaming hot coffee. The rich smell put a smile to my face.

"Cream only for you." She handed me a cup "And two sugars and a heavy cream for you." She passed Damien the other one.

"What are your plans now?" She squeezed against the end of the tailgate and my side. She anchored herself to me and left no doubt which Payne she claimed.

"I'm thinking of reenlisting, but I don't know. I know that I can't do ranch managing even if I hadn't showed my ass all over town, so I need to find something to call my own. Ya know?" Damien sipped his coffee.

We sat for a minute, sipping our coffees, unsure of what to say.

Lexi smirked and laughter bubbled out of her. "You know, this would be the moment Red would have that aha moment."

Her words filtered through and our laughter joined hers. Mull, Richie, and Lionel stopped what they were doing and turned to look at us.

"Yep. That he would."

The laughter stayed bright and loud, but our tears fell, as we grieved a man who had touched us all.

Chapter 34

Lexi sat near the window in the rocking chair. The little baby scrunched her face and protested being shifted before snuggling against the warmth of Lexi's neck and the steady rise and fall of her chest. "Shh," Lexi cooed. Her hand smoothed the tuft of dark black hair that stuck up in every direction. She kissed the wrinkled little face

"Come on. Hand over my niece. I want some of those kisses." Damien gently picked up Rose and switched places with Lexi.

The curtains fluttered in the open window, allowing the fresh breeze of spring to seep into the room.

Monica eased back against the pillows. She winced slightly as the fresh C-section incision tugged against the staples, looking pale but happy.

I sat at the foot of the bed, holding Granddaddy's pipe and surveying the years of memories cluttered around the room.

No one could bring themselves to touch Granddaddy's *toys*, and occasionally, someone intentionally set off the singing fish or brushed against the gurgling self-flushing toilet that lit up.

Rick brought in another cardboard box.

Ethan made a lopsided toddler's dash to Rick. His little arms clung desperately around his daddy's leg and demanded he be picked up. Unhappy with the family's newest unexpected addition, he found every chance he could to be center stage. Happily in his daddy's arms, he scowled at his newest sister.

Julie clung to the edge of the bed and took the couple of steps to Damien in the rocker. Unlike her brother, she stared at the surprise child with wonder and curiosity.

Lexi opened Maw-Payne's top drawer and froze, her hand hovering. "Ren?"

I stepped next to her and tilted my head in befuddlement. The envelope was crisp, and Maw-Payne's flowery writing crossed the front. I set the pipe on top of the dresser. I picked up the letter, turning it over.

"What is it?" Monica asked.

"An envelope addressed to me."

I tipped the envelope to them and walked from the room.

Maw-Payne was a woman of words, but rarely did she write them down.

I sat in her rocker on the porch. The bruise still showed from Donna's attack, but had begun to fade, and the heat from the April sun warmed my tender flesh.

> *Darien,*
>
> *Time is a fickle thing as we learned when Dominick died. I know I will one day join him and sooner than any of you would like. When that happens, I need you to understand why I divided up the Laughing P against what Dominick or even your daddy would have done.*
>
> *Monica, despite being the social butterfly, needs something to call her own. You all do. Since she thought about doing the guest ranch, she is vibrant, assertive, and everything that I knew she could be. And the twins have been a complete blessing.*

The ink had smudged from her fallen tears which permanently stained the paper.

> *Damien has always dreamed of more. He might come home for stints, but he won't ever be content until that boy has travelled the world. Your momma was like that, and it took a good man to calm her. The*

same is going to happen with him, eventually. But he'd never be happy anchored to the ranch with no way out.

You've always loved it here, just like Dominick. I'm putting my faith in him and in you.

I hope that strip of timber gives you and Damien a good starting point on your futures, because life doesn't begin until after twenty-five. Y'all are just now figuring that out.

The rest of the letter was blurry, and I realized tears dripped down my nose, dotting the paper.

Lexi kneeled on the floor, handing me a tissue. She didn't' say anything. Her hair spilled over my lap as she wrapped her arms around my leg and laid her head against my knee.

Shadow's tail thumped against the porch, but he stayed beside Buddy basking in the sunlight.

A few ranch hands hollered their greetings, going to and from the barn. Jason and Jeremy who stood by the trailer, unloading a new water trough for the corral, paused, and Lexi shook her head and waved them off.

I turned the paper over.

I know you don't want anyone knowing this, but I'm proud of what you've learned from Sawyer. I'm glad you had someone to turn to, and so was Dominick. I hope you didn't think we wouldn't find out.

If your sister hasn't found her letter, well then, she hasn't been cooking breakfast. Damien's letter is in Granddaddy's top drawer, next to that pocket knife he got him.

I love you, and I hope you all know that.

She didn't sign the letter, preferring to end it with a flower.

A car door slammed, and Alice hurried up the steps. Her face was pinched with worry. "Is Damien back? Grandpa heard he was, but—"

"He's inside." Lexi leaned back and hollered toward the screen door, "Damien, you've got company."

Alice shifted, and I thought I saw the beginnings of an all too familiar bump. She didn't wait for an invite before opening the door.

The screen slammed against the frame, bouncing twice before settling in the jamb.

"We need to talk." Her voice was stern, and despite my best attempt not to eavesdrop, it was impossible not to with her shouting.

"I was going to call you later or tomorrow. I hadn't exactly figured out what I was going to say." Damien shut the back door, helping with the volume, but the open windows carried their voices just as easily.

With the way Lexi shifted against my leg, I had a suspicion she knew. "You know, don't you?"

She nodded her head. "She called me when she found out a few weeks ago."

Waiting for her to continue was like waiting on Sawyer to finish a story. The pair of them enjoyed taking their time.

"I told her he'd be back when he knew what he wanted from life, and Easter was going to be a beautiful weekend to visit."

I eyed her, wondering how she knew he'd be home.

"Don't give me that look. I didn't know he'd be home. I knew she didn't need to be alone for the holidays, and well, she's part of the Payne clan now. It's what Maw-Payne would have wanted."

I tugged on Lexi's hand, pulling her into my lap. I kissed her hands, nestled within my grasp.

I rested my palm against her stomach, thinking of spring and all the life that blossomed before me.

A part of me was jealous that Monica had another addition and hadn't even known it, chalking up the warning signs to stress over Damien and Maw-Payne. And now, Damien would be a father too.

"Hey." Lexi cupped my jaw, forcing me to look into her sea-green eyes. "Don't go getting baby fever," she playfully scolded. She kissed each of my cheeks, the tip of my nose, and my forehead before kissing me lightly on the lips. "I'm going to enjoy all the time I can with just you before we add another strong-willed Payne to this family." She nibbled along my earlobe. "I'm greedy like that."

Tit for tat, I kissed her neck, tracing the length of her neck with my hand before wrapping my hands in her hair. "Greedy? Insatiable is more like it." I captured her lips, and reveled in the moan that escaped her. "Think you can make it home?"

She shook her head and breathlessly whispered, "No."

I captured her lips again before leading her to the barn.

END

Thanks for finishing *Never too Late.*

If you have a moment of time, could you leave a review on Amazon, Goodreads, or any other site you frequent? It could be as simple as "I liked it." It's the easiest way to help new readers find your favorite authors.

http://mybook.to/LPNever

Laughing P

COLLECTION VOLUME ONE

KARI HOLLOWAY

Southern Charm & Small-Town Secrets.

Cracked But Never Broken

Coming home should have been easy for Marine Damien Payne, but between rustlers, a stalker, and his personal demons, love is hard pressed to find a footing on the Laughing P ranch.

Behind the Lens

Lexi's found freedom from a loveless relationship. Trapped in a hunting cabin with her first love, can she find the courage to follow her heart or will she sacrifice her happiness?

Never too Late

Darien Payne has regretted the moment he screwed up for over a decade. Forged under sweat and sawdust, he sets a plan in motion for his happily-ever-after. Burdened with the brevity of life, he must step up on the Laughing P to keep his family together in their darkest moments for the glimmer of light that always shines.

Join the Laughing P crew from the bottoms of despair to their happily-ever-afters and beyond in this collection featuring all three novels and a handful of short stories.

Short Stories included in the Laughing P Collection

Rowboat for Two

Originally published in Love, Lust, & Scary Monsters, an anthology for Muscular Dystrophy.

Journey back to summer loves, and ranch work as a young Payne taste the sweetness of first loves and first kisses amidst the weeping willows.

https://books2read.com/LoveLustScaryMonsters

A Moment of Time

Originally published in Unbound, a Scribes Circle anthology.

Surrounded by trinkets and roses, Chatan and Pam make love while dealing with the constant battles of getting older.

No longer in print.

Pound of Flesh

Originally published in Black Candy: A Halloween Horror anthology.

What happens when one man's desires turn to obsessions.

Determine to gain Lexi's attentions, she becomes an unsuspecting queen in this game of chess as Ralph's obsessions turn deadly.

No longer in print.

White Moth & Clock Chimes and Worth the Wait have only been available in the collection. Taking place after Cracked But Never Broken and Behind the Lens, these two are worth reading in order.

Author's Note

The book may be over, but that doesn't mean the story is. I don't know what the Laughing P family has in store. Will we hear about Dominick, Red, and Chatan? Will we find the missing cousins? Only time has that answer.

You can catch sneak peeks, teasers and more by signing up for my newsletter on my website: kariholloway.com.